FORECLOSURE FATALITY

A LILY SPRAYBERRY REALTOR COZY MYSTERY

CAROLYN RIDDER ASPENSON

PUBLISHING

Severn River Publishing
www.SevernRiverPublishing.com

This is a work of fiction. Names, characters, businesses, places, events and incidents are either the products of the author's imagination or used in a fictitious manner. Any resemblance to actual persons, living or dead, or actual events is purely coincidental.

ISBN: 978-1-64875-912-3 (Paperback)

ALSO BY CAROLYN RIDDER ASPENSON

The Rachel Ryder Thriller Series
Damaging Secrets
Hunted Girl

The Lily Sprayberry Realtor Cozy Mystery Series
Deal Gone Dead
Decluttered and Dead
Signed, Sealed and Dead
Bidding War Break-In
Open House Heist
Realtor Rub Out
Foreclosure Fatality

Lily Sprayberry Novellas
The Scarecrow Snuff Out
The Claus Killing
Santa's Little Thief

The Chantilly Adair Paranormal Cozy Mystery Series
Get Up and Ghost
Ghosts Are People Too
Praying For Peace
Ghost From the Grave
Deceased and Desist
Haunting Hooligans: A Chantilly Adair Novella

The Pooch Party Cozy Mystery Series

Pooches, Pumpkins, and Poison

Hounds, Harvest, and Homicide

Dogs, Dinners, and Death

The Holiday Hills Witch Cozy Mystery Series

There's a New Witch in Town

Witch This Way

Who's That Witch?

The Angela Panther Mystery Series

Unfinished Business

Unbreakable Bonds

Uncharted Territory

Unexpected Outcomes

Unbinding Love

The Christmas Elf

The Ghosts

Undetermined Events

The Event

The Favor

The Magical Real Estate Mystery Series

Spooks for Sale

Selling Spells Trouble

Cloaked Commission

Other Books

Mourning Crisis (The Funeral Fakers Series)

Join Carolyn's Newsletter List at

CarolynRidderAspenson.com

You'll receive a free novella as a thank you!

To Jack
For always believing in me

CHAPTER 1

*S*ome days started off with a bang, and for poor Alice
Crowder, some days ended with one too.

Belle and I arrived at the Crowder home for our appointment
at twelve-thirty on the dot. Some considered that late, but for us,
it wasn't. The garage door was wide open, but there was no car
inside or on the driveway. Alice Crowder drove a Bramblett
County school bus, and I knew some of the drivers took their
buses home on their split shifts. They usually parked them on
their land, but Alice Crowder lived outside of town, where the
lots weren't large enough. Either she wasn't home yet or she'd
forgotten to close the garage door before leaving that morning.

Belle, on the back end of a sinus infection, cleared her throat.
"That's odd." Her voice came out scratchy. "Why is the garage
door open, but there's no car inside? Doesn't Alice drive?"

"She drives for the schools, remember? Maybe she's running
late?"

She pointed at the front door. "And why is the front door
open?"

"Yeah, that's a little odd." I was also suffering from the begin-
nings of a possible sinus infection, my stomach upset from what

I assumed was sinus drainage. It always gave me a tummy ache and heartburn.

She dug into her leather purse for her phone. "Something's not right. I'm calling Matt."

We'd scheduled an appointment with Alice Crowder to discuss putting her home on the market. Alice said she and her husband Bud had struggled to maintain the mortgage after Bud lost his job at one of the chicken plants in town, and she thought it was the right time to downsize. Bud did get a new job as a truck driver for another chicken plant—there are plenty of them around north Georgia—but his salary was significantly lower, and even with Alice's part-time gig, they struggled to catch up.

Before Belle had a chance to complete the call to her boyfriend, Deputy Sheriff Matthew Riley, Alice Crowder's son Buddy ran screaming out the front door. "Help! My mom's been shot! Somebody help!"

Belle quickly called 911 as I pushed my car door open and rushed to the boy.

"She's...someone shot her!"

"Take me to her," I said as we ran into the home.

Alice Crowder lay face down at the bottom of the stairs in their split-level home, a puddle of blood beneath her. I approached her quickly but cautiously, though her blood splattered all over me from the pressure of my feet hitting the wood floor regardless. I checked her wrist for a pulse, but couldn't find any. When I went to check her neck, I saw the bullet wound in her head and swallowed hard.

Buddy hovered close by. "Is she alive?"

I flipped around and looked up at him. Tears dripped down his face, and his bangs were sticking to his forehead. "Buddy, go back outside and wait for the ambulance."

He stood, feet frozen above his mother's blood, his eyes fixed on her.

"Go! Now!"

His eyes widened, but he turned around and charged up the stairs to the front door.

Alice Crowder's blood was everywhere. Her head lay to the side, and I didn't want to touch it for fear I'd damage the crime scene even more, but I had to check her neck, I had to see if I could feel even the faint beating of a pulse.

I pushed my two fingers gently into the side of her neck, but it was too late. She was gone. I sat there, Alice Crowder's blood soaking through the knees of my jeans, as the soft sound of distant sirens grew louder.

"Lily?" Belle called from the front door. "What's going on?"

"Keep the boy out there, okay?"

"Are you okay?"

"I'm fine. Just keep him outside."

Two paramedics arrived first and rushed in, prepared to save her.

"She's gone," I said pressing my fingers to my head and pulling my hair into my fist. "I couldn't find a pulse at all." I stood with my body pressed against the wall, giving myself a view of the crime scene as well as the stairs. Right now, my biggest concern was my husband.

When you're married to the county sheriff and you have a tendency to be around dead bodies, it causes a bit of a rift in the relationship. That rift wasn't big, but if I wasn't careful, it would be.

As the two men examined Alice, a deputy, whose name escaped me at the moment, lightly grabbed my shoulder. "Mrs. Roberts, come on. Let's get you outside."

"Sprayberry," I said, though I had no idea why that mattered at the moment. "I still go by Sprayberry."

"Yes, ma'am." He helped me up the stairs in time for Dylan to arrive and see me covered in blood.

Great. Just great.

As much as Dylan loved his career, he was a husband first. He knocked the deputy aside and examined me carefully. "Lily, are you okay? What happened?"

The panic and love in his eyes hurt my heart. I hated worrying him like that. I didn't want him to focus on me, though, so I pushed away, knowing he had more important things to deal with. "I'm good." I flicked my head backwards, feeling my blood-soaked hair heavy on my back. "She's been shot in the head. She didn't make it. I was too late."

He held my shoulders and squeezed, glancing behind me at the horrible scene. "It doesn't look like you could have saved her anyway. I'll be out in a few minutes." He eyed the deputy. "Get her to the ambulance."

"Yes, Sheriff," the deputy said.

I shook my head. "I'm fine. Where's the kid? I want to check on him."

The deputy pointed to the ambulance. "They've got him."

A crowd had gathered on the street like they always did when something bad happened in Bramblett County. Two deputies were keeping the rubberneckers at bay.

I rushed over to the ambulance and a teenage boy in tears and shock from seeing his mother dead. Another nail in my heart. Belle was there with him, sitting on his right.

"Hey," she said. "You okay?"

"I'm fine."

Billy Ray Brownlee, a volunteer paramedic, appeared from inside the ambulance and handed me a cup of sweet iced tea and a towel. "How you doin', sweetie?"

"I'm fine, Billy Ray. Thank you."

Billy Ray's job was more victim comfort than actual paramedic. He'd been volunteering since before I was born, and though he'd long ago retired, they kept him on when he felt the urge because he had a way of comforting the injured. He believed a cup of iced sweet tea and a band-aid were the cure-all. He didn't realize it was the sweetness and love of the man who provided them, not the items themselves. I thanked him for the towel, stepped to the side of the big van, and wiped as much blood off as I could. I didn't want to traumatize Buddy Crowder any more than he already was. Then I climbed into the ambulance. "Buddy." I sat next to him and put my arm around him. I eyed Billy Ray and Belle. "Can we have a minute, please?"

"Sure, Lily," they said in unison.

"She's dead, isn't she? Oh God." He buried his face in his hands. "Why? Who would kill my mom? I don't understand!"

I pulled him into a hug, not worried about the blood because it was all over him too. "I don't know, but I promise you, we'll find out."

∾

A gallon and a half. That's how much blood the average human body has, and a good portion of Alice Crowder's pooled on that floor beneath her now covered me. I peeled off my blood-soaked clothing one piece at a time and stuffed them into a plastic garbage bag. I would have thrown them away, but I wasn't sure if Dylan would need them as evidence.

I stared at myself in my bathroom mirror. Not only was Alice's blood on my clothing, it also coated my hair, drying it into matted, knotty clumps. Streaks and splatters of red covered my face like a mask from a horror movie. I'd already turned on the shower, kicking up the heat as high as it would go. When steam filled the bathroom, I cut the temperature just a touch and stepped into the tub. I let the water consume me, let it beat onto my head and race down my body. I kept my head down and eyes open, watching Alice Crowder's life swirl down into the tub drain, then washed my hair twice and scrubbed my body with my exfoliating gloves until I was red and sore. I needed Alice

Crowder's life erased from my body, even though I couldn't erase it from my brain.

I knew I wouldn't be able to sleep or do anything until I heard from Dylan, so Bo and I snuggled together on the couch and watched the Hallmark Channel. I tried to pay attention, but seeing people happy and falling in love after the day I had wasn't easy. Bo rested his slobbery Boxer jowls on my leg, and the thick drool soaked through my sweats, reminding me of Alice Crowder's blood. When he propelled from the couch with amazing force, likely bruising my legs in the process, and ran to the door, I knew my husband would soon walk in. Bo heard Dylan's car a block away, and that wasn't an exaggeration. The dog could hear an ant a mile away.

It was past midnight, meaning it had been eighteen hours for my sheriff husband.

Dylan untied his military green tie and tugged it out from underneath his shirt collar. After unbuttoning the first few buttons of his shirt, he pulled it out from his pants and let it hang, then got comfortable next to me on the couch.

"How you feeling?"

I lay on our gray oversized pillow and didn't look at him. "I'm fine."

He tilted his head. "Let's try this again. How are you feeling?" He slowly enunciated each word.

I mimicked his tone. "I'm fine. I promise. Just tired." I sat up and scooted closer to him. "What happened there, Dylan?"

"Looks like a case of bad timing. She walked in during the middle of a robbery and was shot. We checked the rest of the home, found her purse open and her wallet out. If she had money in it, they probably took that. But other than the car, and maybe some cash, that's it. Probably got spooked after shooting her and took off."

"Really? So you think the car was stolen? My first thought

was suicide, but her car wasn't in the garage, so I guess that makes sense."

"That's our guess, but do me a favor, keep that to yourself. We're not releasing that information to the public."

"You don't think it'll get out?"

"I hope it does, just not from us. I'd like to hear what's said about it, and who says it."

"Got it. She definitely didn't kill herself then."

"Most suicides don't shoot themselves twice."

"She was shot twice?"

He nodded. "Once in the hand and then another time in the head. Looks like she walked in and the unsub held the gun up to shoot her, and when she raised her hands in defense, they shot her hand first. I'm assuming, and we'll know more after forensics gets back to me, she stumbled then, and they shot her in the head. The way she was lying, looks like she was bent over for the second shot."

"That's awful."

"Yeah. It is." There wasn't much he could add to the tragedy of it all.

"Do you have any leads?"

"We've taken down everyone's statement, except yours, and I'll have my deputies hit the street again tomorrow to talk to the people who weren't home today."

"Yes, because everyone knows something, even if they don't know they know it."

A slow grin appeared on his scruffy face. "You actually do listen to me."

"Only when it's about the process of an investigation."

He laughed. "Not surprising. We'll work on your listening skills when I tell you to stay out of those investigations."

"It's a little hard when I'm thrown into them like that."

"Hard, but not impossible."

I sighed. "Can we have this discussion another time? I just

want to know what's going on. I've seen dead bodies before, but this? This was different."

He looked me in the eye, and I saw a mix of love, empathy, and maybe a touch of frustration too.

"So?"

"You know what my mother would say to that."

I rolled my eyes. "Buttons on your underwear. Zippers are out of style, and you're stalling."

He genuinely laughed. "I'm sure we'll say it to our kids one day too."

"Nope. I've already got enough southern sayings burned in my brain from my mom. The last thing I need is your mom's floating around in there too." I nudged his side with mine. "Please. What did he say?"

"Buddy and his friend walked home from school, saw the garage open, but didn't think much of it. Figured Alice had left and forgotten to shut it. They walked inside and a few minutes later headed downstairs to play video games and that's when they found her."

"Did you specifically ask Buddy about the car?"

He nodded. "Said he didn't know where it was. Also said his buddy Hank was there but took off before you arrived."

"He must have because I didn't see him." I thought about what I'd have done if Belle found her mother dead. "I know he's a kid, but way to be there for your friend."

"I thought the same thing."

"It's a school day. Why were they home early?"

"Standardized testing for high schoolers, and seniors had a half day."

"Did anyone talk to Hank?"

"Matt sent a deputy over, and we've got the tri-county area keeping an eye out for Alice's car."

"What about her husband?"

"Buddy said he thought his dad was at work. We're looking into it. Haven't been able to find him yet."

"So, what happens next?"

"We work the case."

"I know, I mean, what are you doing next?"

Dylan adjusted his position on the couch, and I watched as he straightened and then stiffened his shoulders. "Working the case, and that's all you need to know."

Dylan and I'd married a little over two years ago, after an on-and-off relationship starting in high school. We'd separated in college when he disappeared to Atlanta to be a police officer. I thought I'd moved on, gotten over the one that got away, but when he waltzed back into town as the new Bramblett County sheriff, I realized I hadn't.

It took a lot of hard work on his part, and a decision to trust his feelings on mine, for us to revisit coupling, and when we did, it was like we hadn't missed a moment together. We just knew we were meant to be. We knew long before, but kids are stupid sometimes, and young adults don't always have the wisdom to know what's right either, so it took us a bit of time to figure it out.

The first time I saw him officially as Bramblett County's sheriff was when I'd discovered one of my clients dead on her floor. I'd done my best to avoid him, but when I found poor Myrtle Redbecker on her kitchen floor, I had to call 911.

Life had a way of repeating itself.

And so did Dylan's theory that I should stay out of his investigations.

As if he actually thought that were possible.

He groaned. "I'm investigating a murder robbery, and hoping, God willing, my wife will keep her beautiful little nose out of it."

I smiled. "You think my nose is beautiful. Thank you."

He narrowed his eyes at me. "Lily, you promised."

"I promised to keep my nose out of investigations you talked about at home. I didn't promise anything about murders involving me."

He kept his narrowed eyes and furrowed brow aimed right at me. If looks could kill, he'd have been planning my funeral right quick. "Are we seriously going to go through this again?"

Several months ago I might have been involved in a situation that included a gun aimed at me. Dylan, however, continuously forgot how I was able to defend myself. Besides, he taught me how to use a gun, and for over a year I've been at the range once a week improving my skills. And not because it was fun. I did it in case I ended up on the wrong side of a killer's gun again. Because given my track record, the chance of that happening was higher than a hooker holding an aspirin between her knees.

"You can't expect me to walk away. I was there, Dylan. I saw her. I've never seen anything that awful in my life."

"All the more reason for you to stay out of it. You've got enough going on anyway."

I straightened my back. "Other than work, I don't have anything going on."

"You're dealing with the new Hatfield and McCoy battle of the century, for starters. Not to mention you haven't felt well for the past few days."

I shook my head. "I'm fine. It's just sinus drainage, and Bonnie and Henrietta will be righter than rain before we know it. Besides, I am not getting myself in the middle of that mess."

"Right."

"I'm serious."

'You already are."

"Okay, so I am, but that's not because I put me there."

He smirked. "Let me handle this, and you handle the real estate market, okay?" He kissed my forehead and stood. "You coming?"

I mumbled something I wouldn't dare say around my momma.

Dylan said, "I heard that."

I watched Bo act like I didn't exist, following the alpha in the house instead. "Traitor."

My body was exhausted, but my brain was on overdrive, and there was no way I'd fall asleep with thoughts of Alice Crowder and my husband bouncing around my brain. I understood Dylan's request. I knew he worried about me. It was his idea to train me to use a gun, but I was pretty sure he thought the chance of me actually needing it was slim. When he found out I had one pointed at someone's head recently, his theory changed. His newest worrying-about-Lily obsession was that someone would take my own gun and use it against me.

He knew he couldn't keep me wrapped up in a bubble far away from danger, and I don't think he expected that. He expected me to keep my promise and not stick my nose into his investigations. And I had. But Alice Crowder was different. I hadn't stuck my nose in that intentionally. I crashed right into it, and for me, that made it personal. I knew if I didn't do something for Alice, for her son, I'd never be able to live with myself. I also knew if I did, I'd risk building a big wall between me and Dylan.

But we'd had walls between us before and they'd always come down.

CHAPTER 2

*D*ylan was up and gone before my eyes even considered struggling open. He'd left a note on the counter. *Took Bo to day care. Not sure when I'll be home. Love you.* I kissed the note and put it in the mail basket. I'd acquired a box full of his little notes. It was the little things like that I adored most about my husband.

Business was booming, and I had plenty of work to do, so as much as I wanted to hide from the meddlesome eyes and ears of the locals, I had to get to it.

I parked in a spot right in front of the office and carried my laptop bag and purse a few doors down to Millie's Café. Belle was already there, sipping on a chai mocha latte, Millie's latte of the month. I sat across from my best friend and business partner.

Millie offered me a cup of coffee, but the thought of it made my stomach jump. "How about a tea this morning instead?"

"Comin' right up."

"So?" Belle asked.

"Buttons on your underwear. Zippers are out of style?"

"Oh good gravy." Her tone bled frustration, but her smirk told me the opposite.

"I have been strongly encouraged to keep my nose out of it."

Belle belly-laughed. "As if."

"Right?"

Millie walked over with my chai tea. "What are you heifers talking about?"

Belle's eyes shifted toward me. "Did she just call us fat?" She knew what heifer meant, but she liked to needle the woman.

"If y'all are fat then I'm George Strait." She hummed the chorus to "Ocean Front Property" as she scooted away.

Belle wiggled her eyebrows. "I kind of wish she was George Strait. Man still looks fab, and boy, can he sing."

"She's in his fan club and got his new CD. She's been playing it in the kitchen for a week now."

"We should find her a poster of him, you know, from the '80s. She'd love that." I appreciated Belle's effort to keep things casual.

While Millie helped another customer, I switched the conversation back to Alice Crowder's murder. "Did Matthew tell you anything?"

She leaned back in her chair and waved her hands. "Oh no. No, no, no. You are not dragging me into your marital problems."

I flinched. "I don't have marital problems."

"I've got some ocean front property in—"

"Stop." I crossed my left leg over my right, hoping I didn't look as concerned as I felt. "What makes you think Dylan and I are having problems?"

"How many times do you expect that man to put up with you doing the exact opposite of what he asks?"

I jutted out my chin. "I'm not doing that." My shoulders sank. "Okay, so maybe I am, but you make it sound so harsh, and I have my reasons."

"I make it sound like it sounds. He's been asking you to stay out of his investigations since the day he moved back to town, yet there you are, every single time, knee deep in it all. And don't use your reasons as an excuse. People find dead bodies all the time and don't go trying to find the person responsible."

"First of all, it's not been since the day he moved back, and it's not every single time either. Only the times that include me."

"You can call a jackass a donkey, but it's still a jackass."

I didn't take offense to the double meaning of the old southern saying. "Alice Crowder's different. I was there. I literally have her blood on my hands."

"Had. You *had* her blood on your hands, and it's gone now. You can't manipulate a saying to suit your needs much like you can't justify going against your husband's wishes because it suits you."

Before I had a chance to say anything, the café door swung open, and Henrietta Harvey burst in.

"Hey, y'all!" She wobbled over to our table, her yellow potato-sack-style dress swishing against her pantyhose.

Henrietta always wore pantyhose, even during the sweltering days of summer. She once told me the only way to keep what God gave her from hitting the floor was to squeeze it together like a tube of toothpaste. I've never been able to erase the picture of sweet Henrietta walking around with toothpaste tubes for legs.

Millie was bent behind the counter, but heard the familiar southern drawl of one of the two women she called "old biddies." The entire town heard Henrietta. She'd never accomplished the whole inside-voice thing. "Well, look what the cat drug in."

Henrietta sat between me and Belle and held up her palms. "You know how I take mine, roomie."

Belle and I exchanged *oh crap* looks, afraid of what might happen next.

Millie poured a cup of coffee and all but slammed it on the table in front of Henrietta. "We aren't roomies. I'm just letting you stay with me because your best friend kicked you out." She grabbed a hold of my shoulder and squeezed. "Lord knows I get it now. You're about as useless as a steering wheel on a mule."

Ouch. Who knew Millie had that kind of grip?

Belle kicked my leg under the table. We eyed each other with opposite brows raised.

"Awful what happened to Alice Crowder, isn't it?" My desperate plea to change the subject worked.

"Horrible," Millie said.

Henrietta gave us her take on the town gossip. "Heard someone took a sawed-off shotgun to her head and her boy found pieces of it all over the house."

Belle's mouth dropped open.

I leaned forward, bracing my hands firmly on the tabletop. "That is not true. Who's spreading that kind of gossip?"

"It ain't gossip. I heard it from Chubby Henderson at the post office, who heard it from one of his customers who said she lives down the street and saw the brain splatters on the neighbor's window." She made the cross sign over her heart. "Terrible, what happened to that poor woman, and her son, to boot."

"First of all, it happened on the lower level, right next to the stairs, and there wasn't a window near her. Secondly, she wasn't shot with a sawed-off shotgun, and her head wasn't in bits and pieces all over the room. When I saw her, it was completely attached to her neck. I have a mind to tell Chubby Henderson to shut his trap if he doesn't hear it from the sheriff."

Everyone stopped and stared at me, and by everyone, I meant the entire café. Granted, there were only two others in the place, but still. I hadn't realized I'd spoken so loudly or with such emotion.

I tilted my chin upwards and sipped my tea. "Spreading gossip is awful, especially about the dead, and you all know that."

"I'd ask what's got your undies all up in a wad, but seeing a dead body tends to do that to people," Henrietta said.

Bonnie Bass, Old Man Goodson, and Billy Ray Brownlee

walked into the café then, and the collective groans from Belle, Millie, Henrietta, and me were loud enough to make the table vibrate.

Henrietta crossed her arms over her chest and said something ugly. Belle kicked me under the table again.

Three weeks ago, during a typical Georgia thunderstorm, lightning struck Henrietta's home, leaving a gaping hole starting at the roof and stretching down to the ground. The strike had so much power it tore through the siding, framing, and drywall, leaving the neighbors seeing straight into her bedroom. I shuddered at the thought. Thankfully, Henrietta wasn't home at the time, but she couldn't stay there until the repairs were finished. They should have been done already, but the repair team found some mold in the siding, so we encouraged Henrietta to have it all replaced. Had we known what that would mean, and what it would lead to, we would have kept our mouths shut or found another solution.

Bonnie graciously invited her best friend to stay with her and her grandson, and all went well the first day. The next day, and the several that followed, however, were the start of round two for the Hatfields and McCoys.

And everyone in town suffered because of it.

Henrietta complained Bonnie was a slave driver, and Bonnie argued Henrietta lived like a slob. Their fight escalated, causing half the town to pick sides, even betting on the winner—because everyone in town loved to get involved in everyone else's business—and after a few more days, Bonnie kicked Henrietta out on her big fat booty—her words, not mine. And I mean kicked in the almost literal sense. She kicked her in the leg, and told her to get the bleep, bleep, and another bleep out of her house and don't ever come back. I'm sure had she been able to kick her two feet off the ground, she would have reached Henrietta's booty.

Millie and Buford felt bad for her, and offered Henrietta their spare bedroom. Two days later, Millie, with a newfound understanding of Bonnie's side of the story, hopped over to her side. She hadn't made that public, and she hadn't kicked poor Henrietta out, but her patience with the woman sat miles south of gone.

Henrietta sneered at her best friend/archnemesis and said, "That woman's dress is uglier than sin."

Belle placed a hand over Henrietta's. "Don't be getting ugly now."

It was ugly, but I thought it was brave too, especially when Henrietta shot that sneer toward her. I'm not sure I'd mess with either of them even though they were several years older than me.

"Lord have mercy." Bonnie sat at the table next to us, making eye contact with first me and then Belle. "I shouldn't have to say this. I'm sure your mommas taught you right, girls, but you know a lot of good flowers get chopped up by associating with weeds. You might could consider that next time you see that good-for-nothing homewrecker."

Henrietta stood, and as she began to wobble toward the other table, Belle grabbed her arm.

"Don't."

"She called me a homewrecker. Her home was already wrecked when I moved in!" She wiggled her finger at Bonnie. "You better mind yourself before I jam your own business up your hokum-tush."

Old Man Goodson and Billy Ray Brownlee, the ladies' semi-alternating boyfriends, hadn't taken sides, instead choosing to continue taking turns offering support to each of them. It might have been out of fear, but no one in Bramblett County would fault them for that.

Knowing the first punch was just thrown, both men asked for their coffees to go. As Billy Ray tried to pay Millie—she never took his money, ever—Old Man Goodson gathered a barrel full of guts and surprised us all. Not much Old Man Goodson did surprised me, not after the things I'd learned about him, but standing up to those two women? That took a bag full of guts and a truckload of manure, as my momma always said.

"You two ladies are our friends, and we don't want to see neither of you hurt, but if you don't start acting like the ladies we know you are, then you can just go and find yourselves some new men down at the old folks' home, you hear?"

Belle had just taken a sip of her latte, and the shock of Old Man Goodson's comment sent it spraying from her mouth. Normally, I would have said something about that, but I couldn't. My mouth had dropped to my chest and locked itself there.

Bonnie and Henrietta glared at the man and then quickly transferred that glare to poor Billy Ray, who was standing there shaking.

"That how you feel?" Bonnie asked him.

Henrietta told Bonnie to hush herself, and Billy Ray edged closer to Old Man Goodson, not daring to answer the question. He and Old Man Goodson walked out of the café, leaving all of us shocked and a few of us darn proud.

Belle cleaned up her mess. "If that wasn't a duck fit, I don't know what it was."

It was my turn to kick her under the table.

"Bonnie, why don't you come sit with us?" I patted the empty seat next to me. "This has been going on for too long. You two are friends and it's time you work this out. Let's figure out a way to do that, okay?"

She heaved herself out of her chair and yanked her purse up over her shoulders. "I got me better things to do than figure out how to be friends with that snake. And if y'all can't see how awful she is"—she paused as tears welled up in her eyes—"then you're not my friends either." She marched away, letting the door slam shut behind her.

Belle winced. "Oh boy."

Henrietta stood and adjusted her dress. "Y'all picking her side?"

"We're not picking any sides," I said.

"Sure looks like it to me." She yanked her purse off the table and held it close to her chest. "I got a mind to stop coming here if y'all are going to choose that old biddy over me."

We tried to stop her by repeating that we weren't picking any sides, but she stomped out the door just like her former best friend.

"That went well." Belle took another sip of her drink.

"We really need to help them," I said.

Millie nodded. "I got me an idea."

CHAPTER 3

*M*illie's idea was brilliant, but it would have to wait. I had two client contracts to deliver, and Belle needed to finish some marketing pieces she'd been working on. Besides, her plan required some planning itself, and we needed to spend a little time working through the details. We had one shot to get it right, and one shot to reunite the archnemeses back to besties or else everyone in town would suffer.

I headed out with my contracts and a stern reminder from my best friend to abide by my husband's wishes.

Her marital problems comment hit a nerve. Dylan and I didn't have marital problems. Or did we? Could Belle be right? Could my inability to keep out of investigations drive a wedge between us? I hoped not, yet I still found myself driving by the Crowder house after dropping off the two contracts. And when I knocked on the door, I'd convinced myself it was just to check on Buddy, and really, he probably wasn't home anyway. Who stayed at the house where their mother was murdered?

When he opened the door, I got my answer.

From the looks of the boy, his sleep was fitful at best. His hair, a curly brownish-red mass, was smashed against one side of his head while the other side sprang out in complete disarray. "Oh, hey. You're the realtor. Sorry, I didn't know that yesterday." He stepped outside and closed the door behind him.

"Yes, I had an appointment with your mom."

"Yeah, I forgot. She told me about it." His lip trembled. "You know, before."

The metallic smell of his mother's blood lingered in the air, following him onto the porch. How could he stay in the house knowing his mother took her last breath there, in a pool of her own blood, the memories of that burned into his nasal passages? Just standing outside caused the smell to overwhelm me and brought me back to the moment I first saw Alice Crowder's body.

"I just wanted to check on you. Honestly, I'm surprised you're here what with…" I wasn't sure how to finish that sentence.

"Yeah, I was gonna stay at a friend's, but I'm waiting for my dad to come home."

How awful. "Have you talked to him?"

He shook his head.

That was odd. Your mother was murdered in cold blood, and your dad didn't call to check on you? "I know the sheriff is trying to get in touch with him."

"Yeah, he told me he'd let me know. My dad, he drives a truck for the chicken plant. Hard to get in touch with him sometimes. I tried calling him but it went straight to voicemail."

"Are you eighteen?"

"Yes, ma'am."

At least he wasn't being sent somewhere until they could find his father.

"That's good, the sheriff keeping in touch, I mean." I licked my lips. "Do you need anything?" The more I thought about it, the more I realized his house wasn't safe. "I can give you a lift to your friend's house. I really don't think it's healthy or safe for you to be here."

He shrugged. "Yeah, that would be good. I gotta get my stuff though." He opened the door and headed inside. I followed behind him.

Yellow crime scene tape draped the stairs, the words *crime scene do not enter* printed in black across it. All the deputies carried the tape in their cruiser trunks, and I wondered who had been tasked with putting this up.

While Buddy gathered his things, I slipped off my shoes and ducked under the tape, hesitating as my feet hit each step. I'd already been there, seen what I never needed to see again, yet something compelled me to keep going. I stayed on the last step, not brave enough to enter the room itself. I knew the drill. Even though my DNA was already floating around the crime scene along with dust, the authorities might decide to come back and search for more clues. I didn't need to add anything to throw the investigation off track.

The moments I sat with Alice Crowder flew by in a blur, and I hadn't paid attention to any of the details. I didn't have a law enforcement mind. I couldn't dissect a scene, analyze blood patterns, body positions, or even give an uninformed guess to the why of it all. What I could do, though, was solve puzzles, and I'd learned that most crimes were just that. While Dylan worked from facts, I saw things differently, and there were times he'd benefited from my view. Was offering him something useful going against his wishes?

I closed my eyes and held my breath, begging the metallic stench to disappear, wondering again and again how the teen could spend the night breathing in his mother's death. Finally gathering the nerve, I opened my eyes and made mental notes of what I saw.

Yellow crime scene number cards flanked the room. Some sat on the floor while others hung from the walls secured with silver duct tape. I counted twenty and then recounted just to make sure. I snapped several photos of the room, making sure to include every angle for possible review later.

I'd been watching a true crime TV show featuring a detective in Colorado who solved something like a thousand cases over the course of his career. I'd learned a lot from the things he said. In one episode, he talked about how the number of blood splatters on walls and ceilings could determine how many times a person was stabbed. He hadn't mentioned splatters from shootings, but I imagined a theory existed behind them too.

"Uh, ma'am? You down there?"

I stuffed my phone back into my purse, grabbed my shoes on the third step, and took the rest of them two at a time. I'd been so wrapped up in the scene, I hadn't realized I'd made it all the way to the floor after all. "Sorry, I just wanted to..."

"It's okay. The sheriff said they're done down there. He said he'd give my dad the number of someone who'll clean it." He hitched his bag over his shoulder and stepped through the front door. "Just told me to keep the tape up in case someone tried to go down there. I guess people like to look at that kind of thing."

I had a feeling he meant me. I was also struck by how nonchalant he seemed about the place where his mother was murdered. "Did you want to try your dad again? Maybe let him know where you're going?"

"Uh, yeah. Guess I could leave him another message."

We walked out to my car, and I took his bag and set it on my backseat. He stood next to the car and called his dad. After a few seconds he said, "His voicemail's full. Probably 'cause I left him a bunch of messages."

"Did you tell him what happened?"

He nodded.

"Hop in. Where am I taking you again?"

"To Hank's. His mom said I could stay there, and she doesn't work, so she should be home."

"Okay, I'll drive, you tell me where to go."

"Yeah," he said, and climbed into the car.

Hank lived a few miles away, just off the interstate. The drive gave us a few minutes to talk.

"Buddy." I wanted to ease into the conversation carefully. "I'm really sorry about your mom."

He bent his head and had been staring at his phone since the moment he slipped on his seatbelt. "Thanks."

"When you got home yesterday, was your mom's car in the garage?" I knew what he'd told Dylan, but I felt the need to ask anyway.

He balled his hands into fists and released them. "I think it's at the shop."

"I see." That wasn't what Dylan told me earlier. "Do you have any idea why this happened?"

He kept his head bent toward his phone and shrugged. "Everyone loved my mom." He choked out the words, and I knew he was about to cry.

I pulled into the church parking lot a few feet away. "Buddy, you don't have to be strong. You've gone through something awful. It's okay to be upset."

He lifted his head, and tears streamed down his face. He didn't bother wiping them away. "It's all my fault. She's dead because of me."

"Buddy, no. It's not your fault."

"You don't understand."

"Then help me, help me understand."

He stared at me, his eyes reddening as his lids swelled. "I...I should have been home earlier. If I was, this wouldn't have happened."

"It's not your fault. You didn't know this was going to happen. You can't plan for this kind of thing."

"Why, though? I don't know why someone would do that to her. My mom was the best, you know?" He swiped his sleeve across his nose. "I couldn't sleep last night. Every time I closed my eyes, I saw her lying there." He buried his face in his hands and cried, hard.

I wanted to comfort him, but the best I could do was pat him on the knee. There was no comforting someone who'd found his mother the way he had. And like me, when he went to sleep, he'd probably see the image of her lying in her own blood for many nights to come. "Buddy, I know the sheriff well, and I know he'll do everything he can to find out who did this."

His eyes pleaded with me. "What if he can't?"

"I know he will. Trust me, okay? But he's going to need your help. You have to think hard, and I know this is awful, but you have to replay what happened. Maybe there's something you forgot to mention? Maybe you saw something you didn't realize? Think about it, have you heard your mom arguing with anyone lately? Maybe she complained about something at work, or had a fight with a neighbor or something?"

He closed his eyes tightly, squishing his cheeks up toward them, then shook his head. "I don't...I don't know." His eyes popped open. "Where's my dad? Why isn't he returning my calls? Did something happen to him too?"

I didn't have the heart to tell him what I was thinking. Spouses weren't the first suspect just in crime dramas, they were in real life too. "I'm sure your dad is okay. He probably just, I don't know, lost his phone or something. I'm sure you'll hear from him soon." I hoped I was right. "Are you sure you can't think of anyone who might have been mad at your mom?"

"You don't get it!" He cried even harder. "My dad. My dad was mad at my mom! I heard them arguing last weekend." He swiped his sleeve across his nose again.

I leaned over, popped open my glove compartment, and handed him a tissue. "You heard them arguing? Do you know what it was about?"

"I...I...I didn't hear it all, just that he was tired of it, and he wouldn't take it anymore. What if he did it? What if he killed my momma?"

"Did you tell this to the sheriff?"

He shook his head. "I couldn't. I know I should have, but I just couldn't. I don't want my dad going to jail. I can't lose both my parents."

"It's okay. I understand that, but I really think you need to tell him."

"He's going to be mad. I could be arrested for not telling. I know how it works. I took criminal justice as an elective last year."

The poor kid. He was a wreck, and I made a mental note to find out what the heck the school was teaching these kids. "Listen, I promise you, you won't be arrested, okay? I happen to know a little about the law myself, and that's not how things work."

He looked up at me, his blue eyes brimming with tears, tearing my heart to pieces. "Will you go with me?"

I nodded. "Let's go there now."

"Okay."

The sheriff's office was less than five minutes from the church. Plenty of time to come up with a reason for having the son of Dylan's murder victim in my car, right? As my momma always said, hope sprang eternal.

~

When I walked Buddy Crowder into the station, all eyes immediately stuck to us like glue.

Dylan sat across from us at his desk. I tapped my foot to the rhythm of his pencil beating the large monthly calendar covering most of the wood top. He gave me the same look as when I promise to buy him a six pack of beer but forget.

The squinty-eyed, pursed lips, flaring nostrils look. I knew I was in trouble.

"May I talk to you privately?" he said to me, then smiled at Buddy Crowder. "We'll just be a minute. Can I get you something to drink? Water? Coke?"

Buddy kept his head down, eyes locked on the peel-and-stick carpet tiles. "No, sir. Thank you."

Dylan all but dragged me out into the hallway. I rubbed my shoulder, seriously wondering if he'd pulled it out of the socket. "I get that you're upset, but I don't have time for shoulder surgery."

He tipped his head back and took a deep breath, no doubt counting to ten. I had that effect on him. "For God's sake, Lily. You can't help yourself, can you?"

I hiked my hands to my hips and jutted the right side out. "You can lecture me later. How 'bout for now, we focus on the fact that this kid thinks his dad killed his mom?"

He blinked and put his own hands on his hips. "He told you that?"

"He said he heard them fighting, and his dad isn't answering his phone or responding to his messages, so yeah, he thinks it. Do you?"

He dipped his head down and rotated it back and forth, muttering his thoughts out loud. Those thoughts included words that would have caused my momma to wash my mouth out with soap if I'd said them. I cut him some slack, though. I knew the things he saw deserved a cuss word or two. "We can't find the guy, so yeah, he's a suspect."

I pointed to his office. "Consider how that poor kid feels."

He gave me a half smile as he rubbed the top of his head. Dylan kept his hair high and tight—his words. My daddy called it a crew cut. He'd grown it out a bit every now and again, and I didn't mind, but I preferred it short. It showed his strong, chiseled facial features better that way.

"We'll discuss why you went to see him later."

"Yes, sir." The words hissed through my clenched teeth. I thought it best not to mention the discrepancy with Buddy's comments about the car.

His demeanor switched from annoyed to compassionate as he sat back down at his desk. "Lily tells me you heard your parents arguing, and you're concerned your dad may have had something to do with your mom's death."

"Yes, sir."

"I have some questions for you, but I want you to know we've been in contact with your dad's company, and we're looking into his whereabouts. He's got a scheduled run this morning, and I'm sure we'll get in touch with him."

"So you don't think he killed my mom?"

"It's complicated. I don't want to say he did or didn't at this point."

"Okay."

"Do you know what your parents were arguing about?"

"No, sir. My dad just said he was tired of it, and he wouldn't take it anymore. Then my momma said she didn't care what he thought."

Dylan took notes. "Do your parents fight often?"

"No, sir. I mean, I don't think so." His shoulders sank. "I don't really pay attention."

"You're a teenager. You're not wired to pay attention." Dylan set down his pencil and cupped his hands together, resting his elbows on the edge of his desk. "Do you spend time together as a family? You know, nightly dinners, that kind of thing?"

"My dad got a new job, and he's gone a lot. Comes home on the weekends most of the time. I play video games a lot on the weekends, so we don't do much as a family."

He nodded. "Video games, huh? What's your poison?"

That brought out a smile in the kid. "Fortnite. It's awesome."

Dylan smiled. "I just started playing that. Fun game."

He was fibbing. He wasn't a gamer at all, but I knew he wanted to bond with Buddy, and his efforts paid off.

"Since your dad started this new job, has your mom been away from the house? Maybe spending more time with friends?"

He shrugged. "I don't know. She used to play some card game with the neighbors, but I don't know if she does that anymore."

"Bunco?" I asked.

He shrugged again. "I don't know what it's called."

"When was the last time you saw your dad?" Dylan asked.

Buddy shrank into the chair, his shoulders curling forward. "Uh, when they argued over the weekend. He left then."

"Do you know where he was going?"

"No, sir. Are you going to arrest him?"

"No. We'd like to talk with him though, just like I'm talking to you. The more we know about your mom and her last few days, the quicker we can find who did this to her. Do you understand?"

"Yes, sir." He twisted his fingers into a knot. "Why hasn't my dad called me back?"

Dylan exhaled. "I'm not sure." He paused and took a deep breath. I knew he was considering his next words carefully. "The plant's going to contact me when he arrives for his route." He checked his watch. "Should be any minute now. And I've asked them not to tell him about your mother." He leaned back in his chair. "I lose my phone a lot. Leave it places and can't find it. Does your dad do that?"

He nodded. "Yeah, he's always looking for his phone, and his keys."

"I've done that a time or two with my keys too. Tell me about your mom. Your mom's been driving the school bus for a while now, right?"

"Yes, sir."

"And she only drives for the elementary school?"

"I guess."

"Has she ever mentioned any problems with the kids? Maybe she had to report one or talk to their parents?"

"I don't think so, but I...I can't be sure. Everyone likes my mom. She gets all kinds of presents and gift cards on Christmas and at the end of the year, and tons of those little Valentine's Day cards in February." He stared at the wall behind Dylan. "She puts them up on the fridge."

"Did she ever mention having any problems with the neighbors?"

"No, sir. She talked to them when she'd do the lawn and stuff."

"I noticed the one has a German Shepherd. Did your mom like the dog?"

"Hughey?" He smiled. "He's great. Comes over for treats all the time. Mr. Haines always has to come get him. Mom loves Hughey."

"What about close friends? Do you know if your mom had a best friend?"

Buddy's knee bounced up and down, and his top eyelids sank closer to his bottom ones.

"Uh, Sheriff?" I broke in. "Buddy's been through a lot. Maybe it's best to give him some space now? At least until his dad's home? We were on our way to his friend Hank's house, but stopped here first. He'll be able to get some rest there."

Dylan nodded, asked Buddy for Hank's number, and then jotted it down on the notepad.

On the way to Hank's house, Buddy mentioned something that put his friend right smack at the top of my suspect list.

CHAPTER 4

"**Y**ou got it?"

I drummed my fingernails on the yellowed Formica table.

Millie tapped me on the shoulder. "Lily Bit? You in there?"

"What?" I'd fixed a blank stare on an old photo of Ronald Reagan on the wall opposite us. "I'm sorry. What'd you say?"

"You weren't listening to a thing, were you?"

"No, I wasn't."

"Thinking about Alice Crowder, aren't you?"

I nodded. "Her son, actually. Poor kid. He's been calling his dad since he…since it happened, but he hasn't been able to get in touch with him. How awful is that? Kid finds his mother like that and his dad's MIA."

Belle shook her head. "That's awful. I feel bad for the whole family."

"Me, too."

Millie refilled Belle's iced tea. "Sounds to me like his daddy's on the run."

She and I shared the same thought.

A group of people walked into the café and Millie greeted

them with a loud "How y'all doin' today?" She smiled at Belle and me and said, "I'll be back right quick."

Belle picked at the tuna salad oozing out from the sides of her sandwich. She stuffed a piece into her mouth. "You really zoned out there. You okay?"

"I can't shake something Buddy said."

Her eyes widened. "I know I'm going to regret this, but what'd he say?"

"I suggested he get some rest after I dropped him off at his friend's house, but he said they had plans to go to that auto junk yard on the edge of the county."

"Everyone handles grief differently. Maybe he just wants to keep things normal?"

I bit my bottom lip. "Maybe."

She tilted her head. "I can actually see the wheels turning in your brain. What're you thinking? That you should stay out of your husband's investigation?"

I didn't make eye contact. "Did you hear anything about Alice's car? Like what kind it is?"

She waved her hands in front of her. "Oh, no. Nope. Not touching that with a ten-foot pole. No, ma'am. You are not dragging me into this. I'm not married. It'd be easy for Matthew to dump me."

I laughed. "That's the last thing Matthew would do. He adores you."

She shook her head. "Still not letting you drag me into your little pseudo investigation." She took a bite of her sandwich and talked with her mouth full. "Besides, I only got secondhand information about the car." She swallowed her food. "From Matthew."

"Funny how you can get information from your boyfriend, but my husband won't tell me squat."

"Because my boyfriend knows I'm not going to stick my nose in his stuff."

"What did he say?"

She sighed. "Just that it was an Audi, and the keys were missing, so they figured it was stolen."

"Dylan alluded to the same thing."

"There you go. I'm getting the same squat as you."

"Why would they be going to an auto junk yard?"

"Who?"

"Buddy and his friend. On the way to drop him off, he said they were planning to go to the junk yard. Doesn't that strike you as odd?"

"Not really. Maybe they like to fix cars and parts there are cheap? I don't know. Maybe working on a car is therapy for the kid."

"I don't remember seeing car stuff at the Crowder house. Do you?"

"I was a little busy freaking out because of that whole murder thing. So no, I wasn't paying a whole lot of attention to the garage."

I absentmindedly picked at my ham and pimento cheese on rye sandwich, not really having the taste for it, or anything else for that matter. My sinus drainage was really doing a number on my stomach. "Hear me out, okay?"

"Here comes the ruckus-causing part."

I ignored her. "Buddy and Hank go to Buddy's house early because seniors had a half day. His mom works a split shift, and comes home between them. How she got home is yet to be determined. They walk in and find Alice Crowder dead, and then Hank goes home. His friend is there, a hot mess after finding his mother shot to death, and he decides to go home?"

"You saw her. You think a kid could handle that? I'm not sure I wouldn't have bolted either."

"Okay, fine. I get that. But here's the thing. Seniors got out at eleven, I checked. We had an appointment at twelve-thirty. They live three blocks from the school, yet when we got there, Buddy hadn't called 911, and Hank was already gone."

"Okay?"

"And Buddy said it was his fault. That if he'd gotten there sooner, it wouldn't have happened."

"So what are you saying?"

"It doesn't take an hour to walk to their house from the school. Even if they hung out a bit, I seriously doubt they'd stay at school forty-five minutes. No one's allowed to linger like that these days."

"They could have stopped somewhere in town or at a friend's house. Did you ask him where they went after school?"

"No, but still. There's too much time between school getting out, them getting to the house, and us arriving. A, why didn't they call 911, and B, if they had, say, gotten there just fifteen minutes before we did, how quickly did it all go down for Hank to up and bolt?"

"I don't understand where you're going with this."

"I'm saying the timing is off. I don't think they could have just arrived like he said. There was too much blood on Buddy for him to have just gotten there, and not enough time for Hank to cut and run, not without someone seeing him anyway. He'd have to go the way we came, so we should have seen him on the road."

"Let me guess, you didn't see an Audi at Hank's house, and you think them going to an auto junk yard has something to do with Alice Crowder's car."

"Bingo!" I raised my eyebrows. "And my question is, what did he do with it?"

"Probably nothing, because I doubt he took it, but I bet you're off like a herd of turtles to that junk yard, aren't you?"

"A little faster than that. Feel like going for a ride?"

"Daggum woman, you are going to be the death of me and probably the death of your marriage too."

Millie rushed over as we gathered our things and cut me off from defending my position and my marriage.

"Wait! You can't leave. We didn't even get to finalize my plan."

"We got it, I promise. Just get Billy Ray and Old Man Goodson on board, and we're good to go. We can work out the details later. Belle and I need to run an errand."

"You're working on finding who killed the Crowder woman, aren't you?"

I shook my head with a smile.

Millie whipped her dish towel over her shoulder. "Go on then, get your business handled, and I'll get with the boys. We're going to have ourselves a reunion whether those biddies like it or not."

~

"I f anyone asks, you forced me against my will."

I rolled my eyes. "Got it. I dragged you, kicking and screaming like a toddler, into my car, and I forced you to help me. Everyone's going to believe that."

"I don't care about everyone, just Dylan and Matthew."

"Okay then, that's our story if they ask."

"Thank you. I have a question, though."

"I'll tell them I literally dragged you by the arm."

She laughed. "No, not about that. If you think Hank had something to do with the car disappearing, do you think he also had something to do with Alice Crowder's murder? Because if you do, wouldn't that mean her son was involved too?"

"Honestly, I don't know. I'm not even sure if the car did disappear, or if Buddy's just too upset to think straight."

"That's a valid point."

"At first I thought he acted kind of casual, and him staying at the house overnight seemed weird. But he probably felt like he didn't have anywhere else to go, you know? And then a few minutes after he seemed casual, he was really upset, and it seemed pretty genuine to me. Either he's a great actor, or he wasn't involved."

"I think seeing your mother lying dead in a puddle of her blood would be upsetting whether you killed her or not. You have to consider the obvious, Lily."

I glanced at her while I turned onto the main road out of town. "What's that?"

"That Buddy killed his mother."

"I don't know. It seems so far-fetched, is all."

"Still, it's a possibility. Maybe he didn't mean to kill her or maybe Hank was the one who shot her, and that wasn't their plan? That could be why he was genuinely upset when we got there."

"Any of that could be true." I grimaced and moaned.

"You okay? Your face is kind of green."

I swallowed hard, the sensation of the little lunch I ate coming back to show itself again. "I think I'm going to be sick."

"Oh heck, roll down your window then. This is a new shirt."

I pulled to the side of the road and opened the door. I stepped out of the car and walked to the ditch, hoping and praying I wasn't going to lose my lunch. That sensation of tingling, of saliva gathering in my mouth, hit me hard and fast. I bent forward, and then afterwards, I stood there for a minute, shaking.

Belle walked over. "That wasn't pretty." She handed me a tissue. "Here."

"Thank you." I wiped my mouth.

"You okay?"

I nodded as I wiped the tears in my eyes. My eyes always watered when I got sick like that. "I feel better actually."

"Good, just don't breathe on me. We both can't miss work. There's no one to cover for us, you know, like there's no one to cover for us right now. When we should be working."

She had a point. "How about I take you back to the office? I'm going to follow up on a few things, and I'll be back in a bit."

"What about the junk yard?"

I still planned to go to the junk yard, but Belle was right. She didn't need to risk upsetting Matthew, and we needed coverage at the office. I nodded. "Investigating crimes doesn't pay the bills."

"Wow. You not doing your own mini-investigation. Miracles are real."

"I didn't say that."

"Great. Then I'm changing our split to seventy-thirty."

I smiled as I pulled back onto the road. "Deal."

I sent Dylan a text asking if he'd heard from Bud Crowder.

He didn't show up for his shift.

That's not good. Send.

We're pinging his phone.

Buddy said he and Hank were headed to the junk yard. Might have something to do with her car. Send.

Thanks. I'll get on it. Gotta go. Got a ping on his phone.

Let me know what happens. Send.

At least he didn't give me grief about that.

I picked up a pack of gum at the gas station on the way out, popping a minty piece in my mouth to kill the nastiness left over from earlier. When that didn't help, I stuffed in another two pieces and chewed them down to a gooey mass. After thinking it through, I decided to go to the junk yard later. I didn't want to risk seeing Buddy and giving Hank a heads up that I was onto him. Well, I wasn't exactly onto him, but my gut told me something was up, and he didn't need any indication I might know something he didn't want me to.

Dylan mentioned earlier his guys were out talking to the

neighbors, and since it was later in the day, I figured they were probably done. It wouldn't hurt to head that direction and check things out.

Bunco is a popular game for women who live in subdivisions. In smaller places like Bramblett County where we don't have subdivisions, Bible study groups and the like usually hooked up for the game. If I asked around, I might be able to find out who Alice played with, and maybe get a little gossip about the Crowders' marriage.

Every town had gossip. People in small towns just got it straight from an IV to their ear.

I pulled onto the Crowders' street and parked at the corner. Thirty minutes sitting in my car checking emails and such wasn't nosing into Dylan's investigation. After all, Georgia is a hands-free state, and the sheriff's wife should abide by the laws, right? At least when they worked in her favor.

Families inside town were mostly two-income, so catching someone at home in the middle of the day was tough. The county was growing, and people wanting a quieter life were moving in and either commuting to the city or working remotely, so I hoped a few remote workers lived close to the Crowder house.

My assumption that Dylan's deputies already worked the street was correct. Not a deputy vehicle in sight. Of course, that didn't mean they weren't on their way, but I was pretty sure they'd already made their rounds. Dylan was always on top of things like that. I slipped the car back into drive and crawled up a few houses until I had the Crowders' home in sight.

A black truck sat at the end of the driveway. I couldn't tell for sure, but I thought someone was inside, so I stayed back to watch. Sure enough, a man opened the driver's side door and climbed out. His short stature required him to hop off the truck's side step. I inched my car closer, hoping I could get a look at the guy, not that it would matter. I'd never met Bud Crowder, so if that was him, how would I know?

By asking. The man stood and stared at the crime scene tape now on the ground in front of the door instead of attached to it. The man's arms hung limp at his sides, and his shoulders hunched forward, so he obviously wasn't surprised at what he saw. What would it hurt if I offered comfort to someone who'd just lost his wife? I pulled a folder of market files Belle had printed last week and grabbed one. I assumed Bud knew Alice set the appointment to list their house, but having the paper in hand made me feel better about approaching him. Yes, it was tacky, but it was the best I could come up with right now. I walked up behind him. "Mr. Crowder?"

He turned to face me, and his grief hit me like a brick aimed right at my heart. He stared at me through thin slits, his eyelids red and swollen from crying. "Yes, ma'am?"

I didn't think offering my hand to shake was appropriate. "Mr. Crowder, I'm Lily Sprayberry. First, let me say I am so sorry for your loss. Your wife was a lovely lady."

"You're the woman who was here with…with my boy?"

I nodded. "My business partner and I came to meet Alice about your home."

"What about my home? What kind of partner?"

Oh boy.

"We own Bramblett County Realty. Alice called us to talk about putting your home on the market."

"Yeah, I think I've seen your picture around town." The thin slits opened a little. "We aren't selling our home. Why would Alice tell you that?"

I pressed my lips together and quickly gathered my thoughts. "I think she was just entertaining the idea, maybe?" I wasn't about to tell him his wife told me anything about their financial state. It wasn't my business, and I didn't want to embarrass him.

He just nodded, staring off at something behind me.

"The sheriff has been trying to get in touch with you."

"Yeah, I uh...I lost my phone. Got to work late because of it, but they sent me home. Told me he'd been calling."

"Have you called them?"

"The sheriff? A few minutes ago. I'm supposed to go straight there."

"What about Buddy? Have you talked to him?"

He shook his head. "Don't think it's something I can do over the phone, you know? Got his messages, though. Sheriff wouldn't tell me much, but Buddy's messages, they were awful. It's bad in there, isn't it?"

I nodded. "You should call your son. He's been really worried. He needs you."

"I know, but I got to do this first." He lifted his head and gazed at his home. "But I don't know. I don't think I can go in there."

I nodded. "There is a special cleaning service to help with these kinds of things. Would you like me to call them for you?"

The clouded-over, lost expression in his eyes broke my heart.

"Yes, ma'am. That would—thank you."

I stepped away and contacted the Georgia Crime Scene Clean Up service listed in my phone contacts. When you're a real estate agent, you never know who you might need to call, and I had a variety of business numbers in my phone. "They'll be here tomorrow morning at nine o'clock. You don't need to be here. They said you can leave a key under the front door mat."

He dug his foot into a small pothole in his driveway. "Thank you, ma'am."

"Of course." I shifted my weight from one foot to the other. "Mr. Crowder, where have you been?"

"I...I was in South Carolina on a route."

"Buddy said you left after an argument with Alice this weekend."

He looked at me. "You think I killed my wife?"

"I'm just trying to understand what happened. Seeing your son distraught, I just...I want to help any way I can."

He shoved his hands in his pockets. "It was about the dishes." He rocked back on his heels. "We were arguing about the stupid dishes in the sink. I can't stand them there, and I was always getting on her about putting them in the washer." He tilted his head back and laughed. "We always argue about those damn dishes."

Could that have been what Buddy heard? He did say he didn't hear much, just a few sentences between them, but was Bud Crowder holding back? "Did you tell the sheriff that?"

"Plan to when I go there."

"Mr. Crowder, do you have any idea who might have done this?"

He shook his head and paced back and forth. Three steps. Turn. Three steps. Turn. My stomach flipped; just watching him made me dizzy.

"What about her work? Did she mention any trouble with people there?"

He rubbed the back of his neck. "Everyone loved Alice. She... she never hurt anyone." His eyes pleaded with me for answers. "Why would someone do this to her?"

"I don't know." I treaded carefully, not wanting to upset him and shut him off from talking with me further.

"I need to go inside. I need some clothes and stuff for the hotel." He curled his hands into fists, opened them, and rubbed his palms together. "I don't think I can do it."

"I can help if you'd like."

"I, uh, I don't know." He stared at the ground. "Sheriff's sending someone to get my son. Should be here any minute. Maybe I'll have him go in with me."

"I'm not sure your son will want to do that."

"No, I mean the sheriff."

"Oh, okay. May I ask you another question?"

He nodded, but his attention was still focused on the ground. "Do you know much about Hank?"

"Hank? Yeah, he's not a bad kid. Not now anyway."

"Now?"

"Got into some trouble last year but cleaned up his act." He made eye contact. "You think he's got something to do with this?"

I shook my head. "Your son's going to need a lot of support from his friends. I just wondered if Hank could provide that."

He shrugged. "Alice doesn't think Hank's a good influence on the boy what with him getting into trouble and all, but everyone deserves a second chance, right?"

"Did the sheriff tell you about the car?"

"Said something about it maybe being at the shop, but they're not sure. I need to get my wife's address book. Might have the shop she took it to in there. If that's what she did."

"Would you like me to help?"

He didn't answer. "Guess they think it was stolen. Maybe that's what they did? Followed her home and shot her for the car?"

"It's possible."

"It was a nice car. An Audi. Got it for her last year before I lost my job at Southeast Chicken Plant. Used, of course. Audis are expensive, but I got a good deal."

"I love Audis. Which did you get?"

"A Q5. Cheapest deal at CarMax. She wanted something gray but all they had was white." He wiped his eye. "Wish I could have found her a gray one."

A car engine hummed up the street. I glanced behind me and saw a deputy sheriff driving up the road, straight toward us. I'd hoped to get out of there before Dylan's guy saw me. And I had a few more questions.

I pulled a card from my purse and handed it to him. "I have to run, but one more question. What kind of trouble was Hank in?"

"He stole a car. Seems to be trying to stay on the straight and narrow now, though."

"Mr. Crowder, I'm so sorry for your loss. If there's anything I can do, please call me."

He nodded as he stuffed the card into his back pocket. "Thanks."

I darted down the driveway and to my car before the deputy had a chance to talk to me. Buddy got out of the car and ran straight to his dad. I watched them hug and my heart ached for the both of them.

Disappointed I couldn't talk to the neighbors, I made a beeline for the junk yard. If that darn sheriff hadn't pulled me over, I would have made it too.

CHAPTER 5

*D*ylan's smile spread across the length of his face. "Going somewhere special, ma'am?"

Busted. I sank in my seat. "Not anymore."

He laughed. Surprisingly, his face showed no signs of frustration, only lightheartedness. That usually meant one of two things. His pot of patience was brewing quickly to a boil, and he was trying hard not to show it, or he'd given up. I chose to go with the latter because it was the more positive of the two.

"To the junk yard. Want to come?" I joked.

"How about you give me an hour? I'm heading over to talk to Crowder now."

"Can I come?"

"No, ma'am, but you can wait in your car, if you'd like."

"I'll pass, but thanks."

"Don't go to that junk yard without me."

I pressed my lips together and made a popping sound when I blew air from them. "You suggesting I go with you?"

He exhaled. "You're going whether I say no or not, so you might as well come with me."

"You know, come to think of it, I've got some work I could do in my car. I'll just hang out here until you're done. Sound good?"

He laughed. "I figured you'd say that."

An hour later he tapped on my window. "Come on. Follow me."

I pinched my arm as he walked back to his car. Was I dreaming? If that pinch was any indication, I was wide awake, and in desperate need of a manicure. Sure, I'd wanted Dylan to relax about my need to research situations he might consider his responsibility, but I hadn't expected him to be so laid back about it. He was up to something, and I knew I had to tread carefully so that pot of patience didn't explode.

When we pulled onto the rocky entrance to the junk yard, I knew we struck gold, and any explosion from that pot of patience wouldn't be directed at me.

I balled my hands into fists and waited patiently for my husband to step out of his vehicle and walk over to mine. I checked my watch twice, and by the fourth minute, he finally ambled out of his cruiser and sauntered over to the Audi, checked the front left part of the window, wrote something down, and spoke into the two-way radio on his shoulder. He waited another minute, said something else I couldn't hear, and then finally walked toward me like he had all the time in the world.

I pushed my door open and jumped out, ready to race to the finish line. "What were you waiting for, football season to start again?"

That Audi was the cheese, and I was the mouse ready to pounce on it, but Dylan gripped my arm and steadied me. "Let's wait for Matt."

The corner of his mouth twitched. It always did that, since the day I met him a billion years ago when we played on a beat-up old metal swing set that belonged to my mom when she was a kid. My brothers pushed me so high I panicked, bawling my eyes out, fearing I'd go sailing off the thing into the wild blue yonder. They'd just walked away laughing, but sweet, awkward Dylan Roberts, with his buzz cut then too, calmed me by just standing there saying, *don't kick, it'll slow down on its own.* When it slowed enough for him to grab it, he did. And that was the first of many times Dylan Roberts rescued Lily Sprayberry from near death.

I knew then he was the one.

"Oh. Do you think it belongs to Alice Crowder?"

"VIN verifies it."

"You know the kid who was there with Buddy? Hank something or another?" I realized I didn't know his last name. "He got busted for stealing a car." I pointed to the white Audi. "And he left the Crowder house pretty quick that day."

He nodded. "Hank Dean, and I know. He was a minor at the time of the theft, so his records are sealed, but you know how it goes in small towns. No secrets here."

"Don't I know it. So what do we do?"

"You stay in the car, that's what you do. Once Matt's here, we'll go have a talk with the junk yard owner."

"But I'm the one who told you about the junk yard."

He blew out a breath. "We've already been here once. It's standard procedure to check junk yards for stolen vehicles. One of my guys was coming back later today. I know how to do my job, Lily."

The lid on the pot of patience trembled. It still brewed, but it was closer to boiling. I needed to tread carefully. "Of course. I was just...I just...can I please go with you?" I batted my long eyelashes, as if that would ever work with my husband. "Please?"

He dipped his head back and laughed. "That might have worked on the other guys you dated, but..."

"I didn't really date anyone else, remember?"

He smiled. Matthew arrived and parked next to my car.

"Please?"

"Fine." He sighed. "But do me a favor. Try not to say much, okay?"

"Yes, sir." I clapped my hands but stopped when Matthew stepped out of his car, all sheriff-like, bowed-up and tough-looking.

Matthew was attractive in his own right, just like my husband, but when they walked around in those uniforms, every woman's heart in town skipped a few beats. They were a sight to see, for sure.

Dylan narrowed his eyes and used his stern tone. "Let us do the talking, okay?"

"Yes, sir."

Matt smiled, nodding as he chuckled softly. I flicked my eyes at him and winked.

In retrospect, going to that junk yard on my own would have been flat-out stupid. My daddy always said there are places a lady should never go, and though he never mentioned a junk yard, from the looks of the place, it was probably one of them.

A man dressed in a bluish-gray mechanic suit that clearly hadn't been washed in forever, with an equal amount of grime slathered all over his face and hands, stepped out from a back office and stood behind the counter. He smiled at me, but kept his face emotionless when he made eye contact with my two partners.

"What can I do you for?" He kept his tone light, but the cords of his neck stuck out like a sore thumb. "Need something for the lady?"

The man eyed me up and down, leaving me feeling in desperate need of a shower. I didn't want to ask what he thought I might need. In fact, I shuddered at the thought. When Dylan's chest puffed out and he pushed his shoulders back, I knew he felt something too. Anger.

There are some places a lady just shouldn't go.

Dylan inched closer to me. "That Audi out there, where'd you get it?"

He dropped his head. "Picked it up last night, man. Got the paperwork to prove it." He bent down, groaning as his head dipped below the counter, then pushed himself back up and set a pile of papers on the beat-up Formica top. He mumbled softly to himself as he flipped through the papers. "Here." He aimed the paper our direction and pointed to it. "Came straight from the auto shop off 400."

"What's wrong with it?" Matthew asked.

"Engine. Says the owner didn't have the cash to replace it, so they left it."

Dylan read the paperwork. "The auto shop has to keep it a certain number of days before they give it to you. Doesn't say how long they had it on here."

"If the owner doesn't respond to messages after thirty-six hours, they can junk it."

"Mr. James," Dylan said, looking at the man's nametag, "the vehicle is involved in a murder investigation that happened thirty-six hours ago."

His gaze darted between Matthew and Dylan. "I ain't got nothing to do with what the auto shop does. I just get a call for a car, and I go get it." He swept the paper back across the counter-top. "You got a problem, you take it up with them." He folded his arms across his chest.

"We'll have the vehicle towed to our county's impound. Can you tell me if anyone's been inside it?"

Matthew stepped away and spoke into the radio attached to his shoulder.

The man relaxed a bit, though his jaw was still clenched. "I'm the only one's been here so far, but I can't speak for the auto shop."

"Thank you, sir. Can you do me a favor and keep an eye on it until the tow truck gets here?"

Matthew walked back over. "Should be about thirty."

The man nodded, though he didn't seem all that happy about it. "You plan on reimbursing me for my cost? I got tow fees and the money I paid for the vehicle too."

"You paid money for the vehicle?"

He nodded. "Auto shop don't just let us take 'em. We got to pay five bills for them."

I dragged my front teeth over my lower lip. Did he mean five dollar bills, or five hundred dollar bills, or something else? I needed to catch up on the lingo.

"Does the shop charge five hundred for each car?" Dylan asked.

I got my answer.

"Only the newer ones."

Dylan nodded. "You'll need to discuss your refund with the shop or deal with your insurance company on that."

"Figures."

"I need the key to the vehicle."

Mr. James checked the paper, then walked over to a key rack and plucked the key from number thirteen. At least fifty keys hung on the rack.

"It's all yours."

"Thank you for your time, Mr. James. The truck will be here shortly."

We walked outside. Dylan and Matthew each slipped on a pair of plastic gloves. I stood behind them, not wanting to get in the way, and Dylan tossed me a pair of gloves.

I barely caught them. "For me?"

He nodded. "You know you want to look around, and I know I can't stop you, so I might as well let you help."

My mouth dropped open, and for the first time in a long time, I couldn't speak. I tried, but the words stuck to my throat like a lump of sticky oatmeal. I glanced at Matthew, who flicked his head toward the car. I blinked and put on the latex gloves.

Since I had the smallest hands, they gave me the disgusting job of searching under the car seats. You never know what lives under the leather and metal, or what things have grown other slimy, scary things on top of them. I shuddered at the thought, and the two men laughed as I winced and stuck my hand under the front driver's seat.

They gave me the gross job on purpose.

After all that angst and feelings of impending doom, all I found were two greasy French fries and thirty-seven cents. So much for my first official investigation job with my sheriff husband. Dylan and Matthew didn't find anything either, so at least I had that. I peeled off the gloves, noticing once again how desperately I needed a mani. "What's next?"

The tow truck pulled up just then.

Matthew nodded at Dylan. "I got it, Sheriff."

I smiled. "Does he always call you that at work?"

"I require it of all my deputies."

The little twitch of his lip sent butterflies fluttering in my stomach. "Well, Sheriff, what's next?"

He closed his eyes, tipped his head back, and sighed, a sign of frustration I'd learned many years ago. When he opened his eyes again, he smiled. "Follow me. We're going to the auto shop."

I smiled. "Am I your deputy now?"

His eyes traveled down my body and then back up, settling on mine. He smiled. "Khaki and brown aren't your colors."

I smacked his shoulder.

"Come on, let's go find Alice Crowder's killer."

CHAPTER 6

I bounced in my seat the entire drive to the auto shop. Dylan was actually letting me go with him on a real witness questioning. He probably wouldn't let me say anything, but I didn't care. It was a step in the right direction. We'd gone from stay out of it to come along, and who knew where we'd end up next? Maybe he'd deputize me and then I could officially help? I could become one of those auxiliary deputies, the ones who volunteer and get to do real sheriff stuff, or maybe I could go to the academy? Maybe law enforcement was my thing after all? Dylan and I could open our own private detective agency and be like those people on that show on Hallmark, the Hart Family or something. Except they were super rich, and we weren't.

Dylan's car was stopped in front of me, but I'd been so wrapped up in my little private detective partnership fantasy I wasn't paying attention. I slammed on the brakes and stopped with less than an inch between us. I ducked down in my seat in case he saw through his rearview mirror. Get it together, Lily, or Dylan won't let you be involved.

We arrived at the shop, and I got out of my car as he walked up.

"Nice braking there. It's a big fine, rear-ending a county vehicle, you know." He smiled.

"I'm sure I'd get a discount or something. I have connections."

"From now on, I'm driving everywhere."

"I'm good with that."

We walked over to the open garage. My breath caught when I saw the sign hanging over it. "Dylan, do you see that?"

He nodded.

"That's—"

He cut me off. "I know. Just let me handle it, okay?"

I nodded.

Two men had their heads buried in the engine of a Ford pickup. Dylan and I stood there for a moment, but when neither of them noticed us, he coughed.

The older of the two men—his gray hair a giveaway—wiped his hands on a dirty blue cloth and walked over to us. "Afternoon, Sheriff." He smiled at me. "Ma'am. What can I do you for?"

"I'd like to talk to you about the white Audi you had picked up yesterday."

He nodded. "Sure, come on over to the counter. I'll grab the paperwork."

We walked over, and I pressed my lips together, not wanting to show any excitement in such a serious situation.

He removed a clipboard from the wall and flipped through the pages. "Looks like I got it last weekend. Kept it a few days longer than required, and then had the junk yard come get it yesterday."

I nudged Dylan's boot with mine, but he ignored me. The junk yard said the auto shop had it for thirty-six hours. The stories weren't matching up. I wasn't a professional, but I knew that meant something.

"Who brought you the vehicle?"

He glanced at the paper again. "Nobody. We got a call it was abandoned in the outlet mall. We got an arrangement with property management there. Unless the car is impounded, they call us, and we pick it up."

Dylan nodded. "Then what do you do with it?"

I leaned toward him and whispered, "Why would the outlet mall have it towed to an auto shop?"

The man must have heard me, because he raised an eyebrow. "Was the car reported stolen, Sheriff?"

"It's involved in an ongoing investigation." Dylan adjusted his stance. "So, let me see if I've got this straight. Mall management called and said they had an abandoned car, you picked it up last, what, weekend?"

He nodded.

"Sat on it a few days and then had the junk yard pick it up."

He nodded again.

"When did you make the arrangement with mall management?"

"Oh." He chewed on a piece of gum, smacking his lips together each time his teeth chomped down on it. "About six months, give or take."

"That's some arrangement you got there. The sheriff's office is supposed to be notified of any abandoned vehicles."

The man shrugged. "Ain't up to me, what the mall does or don't do. I just get the call, and I pick up the car. How they choose to handle it is their business." The man's left eyebrow shot up. "This ain't the Crowder woman's car, is it?"

Dylan nodded once.

The man ran his greasy hand through his equally greasy hair. I cringed, knowing the only way to get that out was with a good dose of Dawn dishwashing detergent.

"I...her son is friends with my son. He told me what happened."

"Hank Dean," Dylan said.

The man nodded. "Yeah, he was…uh, he was there, he said. Got scared and ran home. Told him I understood, but he needed to be a man and be there for his friend. Kid stayed at our house till his pa got home. Can't imagine not being there for your kid like that."

"I was there. It was a hard thing for me to see, so I imagine it was awful for your son, too," I said.

"Not as awful as it was for Buddy." He shook his head and glanced down at the stained and chipped countertop. "Hank was so upset. His hands wouldn't stop shaking." He looked into Dylan's eyes. "Your deputy talked to my boy. He told him what happened, yes?"

Dylan nodded. "But the car."

Mr. Dean swore like a truck driver as he paced behind the counter and tossed his hands in the air. I watched, thinking he was lucky I had brothers, because that cussing would have offended most everyone else.

"Mr. Dean, I'm aware of your son's history."

The man interrupted him. "Oh heck, everyone's aware of my son's history. It ain't no secret, but this don't make sense. The car. It was at the out—" He stopped, his mouth hanging open for a moment, and then another round of cuss words trailed off his lips. "That boy. He works at the outlet mall. He said he learned his lesson. He's a good boy, Sheriff. He ain't involved. He can't be."

If I'd learned anything in the past few years, it was that the impossible was very possible, and often likely. The things we least wanted to happen were often the things that did. I had a feeling Mr. Dean knew exactly how that felt.

"We'd like to talk to your son again."

"Does he need an attorney?"

"It's just a few questions, Mr. Dean, that's all."

He nodded. "Sure, yeah. I can, uh…I can bring him in tonight when the shop closes. Will that work?"

"How about if I come by your place, say around eight?"

"Uh, yeah. I'll make sure he's home."

"Thank you. In the meantime, Mr. Dean, I'd appreciate it if you'd keep this between us. If your son knows anything, I don't want to scare him."

"If he's involved, and I ain't sayin' he is, he could be in a lot of trouble, huh?"

"He's eighteen, sir, so he's an adult."

He nodded.

Before we left, Dylan had Mr. Dean make a copy of the car's pickup information. I tried to talk to him outside, but he said to hold off and to follow him. So, I did.

To Millie's.

And when we got there, we both wished we'd chosen someplace else, someplace far from the Hatfield and McCoy feud going on between Bonnie and Henrietta.

~

Old Man Goodson and Billy Ray Brownlee sat with their heads down and shoulders sunk as Henrietta vented her frustration their direction.

"That woman's got more nerve than a rotting tooth. She thinks she can tell me what to do and when to do it? I'm not her little grandson. I'm a grown woman, and a mighty fine one at that."

"You're both mighty fine grown women," Old Man Goodson said, his voice as soft as a mumble.

Bonnie gripped her oversized yellow purse. "Why I oughta..."

It all happened so fast, yet it felt like I was standing there watching a movie in slow motion. The purse flew up and behind her head and then it came flying back, headed straight for the side of Henrietta's head. In three elongated steps, Dylan reached the flying purse, scooped it into his large hand, and whipped it to the ground.

Time stopped. The entire café went silent. That saying "you could hear a pin drop" couldn't describe the silence in the place.

No one moved. I'm not sure anyone breathed either, no one except Dylan anyway. And when he spoke, it was loud and clear. Very clear.

"Enough!" He set Bonnie's purse on the table and stood with his legs spread and his hands on his hips. He tipped his head down and shook it before raising it and alternating narrowed, stern eyes on both Bonnie and Henrietta. The entire café sat frozen, their eyes locked on Dylan in anticipation of his next move. "Haven't you had enough?" He waved his wrist toward Old Man Goodson and Billy Ray Brownlee. "I know these men sure have." He turned to his side and glanced around the café. "And I'm pretty sure everyone else has too." He patted Billy Ray on the shoulder. "Look at poor Billy Ray and Old Man Goodson here, they're a mess. You've dragged them into your little hissy fit and then you get mad at them for not picking sides. Do you think they're crazy?" He blanched, a look that wasn't becoming on him. "No man in his right mind would take sides in this battle. And for the two of you to even expect them to?" He did the head dip and shake again. "I don't know. I'm just ashamed of you, that's all. I expect better of you two."

Bonnie opened her mouth to speak, but Henrietta whacked her on the arm. "Hush, woman, or he might shoot us both."

Bonnie's eyes popped wide open. "He does have a big gun."

Henrietta smiled. "That ain't the only big thing he's got."

"Henrietta!" I wasn't sure whether to laugh or be horrified. "That is not appropriate at all."

She blinked. "What? I'm talking about that bat thing he's got hanging off his belt."

"It's a truncheon," Dylan said, trying hard not to laugh.

"A luncheon?" Bonnie asked.

Dylan pressed his lips together. "A baton."

Henrietta crossed her arms over her chest. "Looks more like a bat to me."

Dylan inhaled a deep breath and let it out slowly. He released frustration that way. I knew it because I'd seen it many times before, mostly aimed at me.

"I'm not going to use my stick or my gun on either of you. Not yet, anyway."

Millie had been standing to the side, probably thinking it was the safest place in the café, giggling. I looked away like I hadn't noticed, afraid I'd chuckle too.

Dylan eyed her and she shut up right quick. "You two have been going at it like grade schoolers for weeks now. It's time you figure out how to solve this…this thing between you two. You either work it out, or find a way to get along in public. If you can't, and you resort to violence like this again, I'll drag your butts to jail and keep you there until you make things right."

Bonnie plopped into her seat and let out a huff. "She started it."

Henrietta's mouth dropped open, and after a few seconds, she spoke. "I didn't start nothing. You asked me to stay with you. It ain't my fault you don't like the way I live."

"The way you live? You can't call leaving your dirty laundry on my bathroom floor living. And my toothpaste? You're supposed to roll the tube from the bottom, not squeeze it to death so it pops out the other end." She mumbled something I didn't hear and then crossed her arms over her chest and stuck out her bottom lip.

And off to the races we went again. I smiled at Millie.

She shrugged. "I got her a tube of her own."

Dylan leaned his head down toward my ear and whispered, "Promise you'll never complain if I leave my clothes on the bathroom floor?"

"I can't do that."

"What I thought."

"But you can eat crackers in my bed anytime."

"Good to know, Barbara."

I smiled, happy he got the reference to the country song. Dylan just got me.

Dylan clapped his hands together and rubbed them before sighing loudly. He planned to make a point, and once again, most of the joint waited breathlessly for him to do so. "Bramblett County isn't big enough for the two of you to be fighting like this."

I raised my eyebrows. Before Dylan could say his piece, the café door flew open, its bell chiming as it hit the wall. The entire café shifted its direction.

Belle stormed in all smiles. "Hey y'a—oh." She hitched her bag over her shoulder. "Did I come at a bad time?"

Bonnie jerked her thumb toward Henrietta. "Any time's a bad time with that one."

Henrietta pushed her shoulders back and lifted her chin. "I'm fixin' to lose my religion on you, woman."

"Oh, my," Belle said. She skirted toward me and set her bag on the floor. "This ought to be good." She flicked her head at Millie and smiled. "Got any popcorn for the show?"

Chuckles and giggles filled the room, but Bonnie and Henrietta sat stone-faced and sullen.

Billy Ray coughed and moaned a little as he shifted in his seat to face Belle. "Miss Belle, our sheriff here was just about to say something."

"Oh, well then, go right ahead, Sheriff."

Dylan shot me a look, the one with his eyes wide and brows raised. Apparently, he hadn't planned to say anything after all. I stepped in, going with a downsized version of Millie's plan.

"Here's the deal." I pulled a chair over between the two sides and sat down. "We're going to have ourselves a meeting. Tonight." I pointed at each of the ladies, including Belle and

Millie. "You get there by half past six." I then pointed at Billy Ray and Old Man Goodson. "You two show up about seven. Okay?"

The men nodded. Two of the women nodded, but not the two I'd hoped. Before I pushed them to agree, Dylan interrupted.

"Lil, I've got an investigation to handle. I'll see you at home tonight. Probably late."

I shot out of the chair. "But I thought we were going to—"

He kissed my forehead. "I've got it. You're needed here. I'll try to come home after talking to the Dean kid."

I groaned. He'd found an opportunity to push me out of his investigation and took it. "Fine."

He winked and then directed his attention back to Bonnie and Henrietta. "Until you two figure how to behave in public, I'm banning you from Millie's."

The small crowd gasped, including me.

"You can't do that," Bonnie said, her tone high, her voice shaky.

Millie chimed in, "You bet your butt he can."

Henrietta huffed. "I don't see why I can't come where my roomie works. That's got to be some kind of abuse of the law."

"I'm not your roomie," Millie said. "You're staying at my house until your repairs are finished."

Bonnie made a harrumph sound. "Looks like even Millie don't want you."

Dylan shook his head. "All right, you two, we're done here. I've got to find a killer, and I don't have time to deal with your hissy fits. Now up, both of you. I meant what I said."

Whatever was on Billy Ray and Old Man Goodson's Formica tabletop must have been very interesting because they both kept their heads down.

Bonnie stood, a slower process than normal for her, and probably a stall tactic. "Fine then. I can go to the drugstore and have me a coffee there. Come on, boys, let's go."

The boys didn't budge.

Dylan handed Bonnie her bag. "I'm also forbidding the boys here from being with either of you. At this rate, they won't want to be soon enough anyway."

Ouch.

Henrietta shimmied out of the chair, one hip at a time.

Seeing the two women's faces, a mix of sadness and anger, and watching them both struggle a bit as they moved made my heart hurt. They needed each other. Their fight was silly, and I planned to make them see that at the intervention Millie thought up earlier. "Don't forget. My house, at half past six. Okay?"

They both grumbled as they headed out the door, side by side.

I looked at Belle and smiled as she held her hand to her chest. We both saw it. Even though they were mad at each other, they bonded together naturally when asked to leave.

That was a start.

CHAPTER 7

*B*elle sipped her coffee. "We need to go outside. Bubba Johnston's farm is close by. Maybe we'll see his pigs flying overhead."

I laughed. "Right? It's a miracle."

"So he what, deputized you or something?"

"I wish, but no. He just let me tag along."

She shook her head. "I'm honestly speechless."

"Now that's a miracle."

"Well? What'd you find out?"

"For starters, the car's been missing for a week, and Hank has a history of car issues, you know, of the criminal kind."

She pressed her lips together. "Interesting. So Dylan thinks he's involved, too?"

"I'm not sure. We were supposed to talk about it here, but then Hatfield and McCoy got all up in arms and blew that chance out the window."

"So, what do you think?"

"I think something's up about the car. I think it's connected."

She piddled with the three chocolate chip cookies Millie

brought out for her, taking one and placing it on top of the other. "What do you mean?"

"I'm not sure just yet, but Buddy knew it was gone. He just wasn't exactly sure for how long or where it was. Just said he thought it was in the shop."

"Interesting." She took a bite of a cookie. "This is amazing. Try it."

"No, thanks." I pointed to my throat. "Still have some sinus drainage going on."

"I guess that's not unusual, a kid not knowing what was going on around his house?"

"I guess."

"Matthew said they talked to the husband?"

"Yeah, but I actually got to him first."

"Of course you did." She bit the cookie again. "What'd he have to say?"

"He seemed genuinely upset. Said he'd been on a truck haul, but I'm pretty sure that was a lie. He also wasn't exactly sure where the car was. He said the sheriff told him they thought it might have been stolen, and then he said maybe she was killed because of the car."

"And you think the car has something to do with it, so that makes sense."

"I can't figure out what, though. There's just too much confusion around the car. For me, that's a sign."

"What about for Dylan?"

"I'm not sure. It's a red flag for sure, but I don't know how big of one. I guess it's pretty big since he thinks she was killed during a robbery." I tapped my finger on the table. "Can you do me a favor?"

"Is it potentially damaging to my relationship with Matthew?"

"Not if you don't tell him."

She shook her head. "Fine. I'm in."

I knew I could count on her. "Can you get a list of the auto shops around town, maybe give them a call and see if they've had a white Audi in the past week?"

"Why? You already know it's been at a shop."

"At one shop, yes, but my gut tells me, I don't know. I just feel like it's been somewhere else. I could be wrong, but what's the harm in checking?"

"Fine. I'm going to need the model and stuff if you know it."

I dug in my bag for my spiral notebook and a pen. I jotted down everything I knew about the car. "Here you go."

"I've got some real work to do first, but I'll make some calls."

"Thank you."

"Oh, by the way, you remember work, right? That stuff we do in the office we rent a few doors down? You know, the whole selling homes thing?"

"I know. I'm sorry. I have a to-do list and I'm working on it."

"Right."

And I was. Knowing Belle was trying to gently make a point, I got my butt in gear and got to work. I had no idea how much I could get done in a short time if I truly focused, and thank God I did. We had two offers on two of our listings, and one client ready to make another. I called our listing clients, gave them the information, then wrote up the offer for the other and sent it off to the agent. With work completed, I felt a lot better about skipping out to dig my hands into Dylan's investigation a little more.

~

The roaring, rough bark of a big dog echoed my knocking.

"Hughey, silence."

The door to the Crowders' neighbor's home opened and a bald man with a Santa Claus belly and a scruffy five o'clock shadow smiled down at me. The German Shepherd sat at his side eyeing me like I was his next meal.

"Well hello, miss. Aren't you a little old to be selling Girl Scout cookies?"

My stomach churned, though I wasn't sure if it was because of the man's creepiness, or the mention of cookies.

"Mr. Haines?"

He nodded.

"Your dog won't bite, will he?"

"Not unless I tell him to."

"My name is Lily Sprayberry. Your dog is beautiful."

"Thank you. He's a good boy. Got him a few years ago."

The dog stayed by his side, and when the man told him to stand, he stood. He gave him a few other commands, and the dog did as told.

"Got him professionally trained by a canine police trainer in Atlanta. Dog can do just about anything."

"That's wonderful. A well-trained dog is a great pet. I have one myself."

"Great protection. What can I do you for today, ma'am?"

"I was at the Crowder home yesterday, and I—"

"Oh, yeah. The real estate agent. Awful, wasn't it? What happened to Al."

"Yes, it's terrible. I was hoping I could ask you a few questions?"

He raised his eyebrows. "Sure. Just made a fresh pot of decaf. You want a cup?"

"That would be lovely, thanks."

Real estate agent marketing 101—always take the cup of coffee. It's a way in and a way to stay in. I had to make it quick, though. I didn't have a whole lot of time before I needed to be home for the B and H intervention.

I stepped inside and straight into a New York City condo. "Wow, this is stunning." I took in the entire living area, a large open space filled with modern furniture in muted grays and creams. A huge flat-screen TV the size of a queen bed hung on the side wall over a white marble fireplace. The dining room table, a glass rectangle on a white metal pedestal surrounded by six white metal chairs, jutted out in the back left corner. The kitchen, wow. The kitchen. Stuff of magazines. White cabinets, white countertops, stainless steel appliances. All things I hoped to have someday. The dining area and kitchen, at the back end of the house, had the best view through quadruple French doors leading out to the backyard. Okay, so the backyard wasn't much to stare at, but still, the entire setup was absolutely stunning.

Mr. Haines stood there proud as a pig in mud. "I get that a lot, that wide-eyed-look thing."

"I can imagine. It's beautiful. Did you...you didn't—"

"Oh, no, ma'am. My wife. She likes those home décor magazines, and one day I came home and she told me she'd cashed in her life insurance policy and hired a designer. Said she didn't need all that money for her to die. I could just dig a hole in the ground and throw her in it. She wanted her fancy house, and she was goin' to get it."

"Kudos to her."

He shrugged. "She died before it was finished. Cancer. She knew she had it but didn't tell me till it was too late. She thought she could make it till the redecorating was done, but things don't always work out the way we want, now do they? Guess she learned a lesson."

"Oh, I'm so sorry."

He waved it off. "Don't be. She's happy it's done. I'm sure she's looking down at me and complaining I don't sweep the dog hair enough."

I couldn't help but giggle.

"Let me get that coffee."

"I'm kind of afraid to drink it. What if I spill?" I laughed, but I was half serious.

"Don't mind it none. A house ain't a home if it's all sparkly and clean."

He had a point.

He set a tray on the coffee table and offered me the sugar.

"Thank you."

"You looking for clients?"

"Oh, no. I'm actually here about what happened."

He raised an eyebrow. "Well, I don't know much. Just that poor Buddy found his momma dead, and old Bud wasn't around to be there for his kid." There was a slight tone of disapproval in his voice.

"Yes, I imagine it's a hard life, being a truck driver."

"Don't know, but that boy needed his dad and he wasn't there. I got a problem with that."

"Did you not get along with the Crowders?"

"'Course I did. Al and the boy, that is. Hughey goes over there and plays all the time. Not sure what'll happen now. Al loved him and he loved her."

"Did you talk to Alice before she was killed?"

"Talked to her every day. She'd come home from her morning route and we'd have a coffee while Hughey ran around." He nodded. "Dog's going to miss her."

Speaking of the dog, he lay on the floor next to the couch, still eyeing me like I looked yummy. He was well trained, though, so I wasn't too worried.

"Did you see her Tuesday?"

"Didn't get a chance. She came home and then left right quick." He blew out a breath. "Come to think of it, she drove off in a hurry too. Came outside with Hughey here and saw the tail end of her car driving away."

"Her Audi?"

"Yup. She loved that car. Said it was the only nice thing Bud did for her in years."

"Were they having problems in their marriage?"

"Who isn't?" He laughed. "Don't think I know a soul who's happy with their spouse, not all the time anyway. Marriage is a compromise. You give a little, take a little, that kind of thing. Only most people take a lot and forget to give. Bud, he's that kind of guy."

"You seem to know the Crowders well."

"Been neighbors a while. Al, she helped after my wife died. Brought me dinners." He smiled. "Boy, that woman could cook a hamburger casserole like them New York City chefs." His shoulders sank. "Hughey sure is going to miss her."

I had a feeling Mr. Haines would miss her more. "I came by on Tuesday because Mrs. Crowder—Alice—wanted to talk about putting her house on the market. Did you know she was interested in selling?"

He shrugged. "I knew she was thinking of leaving Bud, so I guess selling the house would be the next step."

"She told you she was thinking of leaving her husband? Do you know if anyone else knew?"

"I'm not a gossip, and I don't want to start no trouble, but neighbors talk, you know? Word gets out."

I nodded. "Mr. Haines, are you certain it was Alice's car you saw leaving Tuesday? Did you see her driving?"

"Like I said, it was already tail end down the street, so no, I didn't see her driving."

I finished the last sip of my coffee. "Well, thank you. I appreciate you talking to me."

We both stood and walked toward the door.

"Appreciate you coming by. Talked to that sheriff deputy, but all he wanted to know was whether I saw her that day or not."

I stepped outside. "Did you tell him anything you told me?"

"Don't think I did."

"Thank you. I know someone in the department. I can get them the information."

"Sounds good. You take care now. You got a card? 'Case I

decide to sell the place. Not sure I'll get anything for it what with a murder happening next door and all."

I handed him a card. "Sadly, or luckily, I'm not sure which, people forget those kinds of things quickly."

I climbed in my car and jotted down a few things he'd said. He couldn't say for certain he saw Alice's car heading down the street Tuesday, but if it was, that meant someone was lying. And if I had to bet on it, I'd pick Hank's dad and Mr. James at the auto shop.

CHAPTER 8

As I pulled down the driveway, a woman across the street came out in her robe and slippers, walking straight toward her mailbox. I couldn't ask for better luck. Obviously it was a message from God that I was destined to talk to her, so I pulled over and introduced myself.

"Hi, my name is Lily Sprayberry. I was—"

Unfortunately, she wasn't as pleasant as Mr. Haines. "I know who you are. You're the real estate agent with her face all over town. You sure get around, don't you?"

Well then. "Business is good, yes. Um, I was hoping I could talk with you a minute about—"

"We ain't looking to sell anytime soon. 'Sides, who'll want to buy a house across the street from a murder?"

"I'm not asking about your house, ma'am. I'd like to talk to you about the murder."

That got her attention, so I stepped out of my car.

"What's it to you, what happened to Alice?"

"I was with her son shortly after he found her. Let's just say I have a vested interest."

She riffled through her stack of mail. "Suit yourself."

I couldn't have been any more uncomfortable at that moment, and I would have preferred hopping in my car and darting off, but I needed information, and her proximity to the home meant she might be a source for it. "Mrs..."

"Bucklett. Mayme Bucklett."

"Mrs. Bucklett, were you home the day of the murder?"

She finally looked up from her mail. "See the way I'm dressed? Does it look like I get out much?"

Kids at Bramblett County High School went out in their pajamas all the time, but that wasn't a thing for women in her age group, or mine. But seriously, what was I supposed to say to that? "Gunshots are loud, maybe you heard it and looked outside to see what it was?"

"I heard it. Thought it was a car backfiring. That boy down the street has one of them hot rods and it's always popping off like that."

"Then you didn't look outside when you heard it?"

"I didn't see nothing when I checked, but a few minutes later I went out for the mail and saw Alice's car pulling out of the driveway, so I might have heard something, but it wasn't no gunshot. Dead women don't drive."

"You saw the car? Did you see Alice driving?"

She shrugged. "Wasn't paying attention."

"Do you recall what time that was?"

"I come out when I hear the mail truck coming by, so whenever that was."

"Around what time does the mail come?"

"You sure are asking a lot of questions. You might could let the police handle this. Ain't your job anyway, now is it?"

"No, ma'am. It's not, but like I said, since I was there with Alice's son, I feel an obligation to help."

"Bet your real estate customers don't appreciate you taking time away from them."

"Were you friends with Alice?"

"Me?" She pursed her lips. "I like to keep to myself. People like to gossip, and I don't need them gossiping about me."

"I can understand that."

"Bud and my Stew are friendly, though. Matter of fact, Bud came by last week and showed Stew his new gun." She tapped her finger to her chin. "Maybe I should call the police about that?"

"Have you talked to the police already?"

"Nope. They haven't been by at all. 'Course, the day Alice died I had me an awful headache. Took some sleeping pills after getting the mail, so they could have come by and I didn't know it. Them pills make me sleep like the dead."

"I know someone at the sheriff's office. I can let them know you have information. Do you happen to know what kind of gun it was?"

"I don't know much about them kinds of things. Stew's got himself some hunting rifles, but Bud's wasn't big like those. It wasn't much bigger than his hand, but I really didn't get a good look. I make Stew keep the guns in a case 'cause I don't like seeing them around. Things scare me."

"They scare me too."

"If you're telling the police what I told you, you ought to tell them about the affair. In the movies it's always the husband that does the killing when the wife's goin' out on him."

"What affair?"

"'Course, like I said, I don't like to gossip, but yeah, rumors get around, and I heard Alice's been going out on Bud for a few months now."

"Who is she rumored to be going out on Bud with?"

She shrugged again. "You ask me, it's Roger. Man's over there all the time. Dog's always running around loose, scaring people too. You ought to tell your sheriff friend about that too. One of these days I'm going to call the pound and have them come get that thing."

"You mean Mr. Haines's shepherd?"

"Yeah, Roger." She retied the belt on her robe. "That all? My show's 'bout to start."

"Oh, yes. I'm sorry to have kept you. Thank you for the information, and I'll definitely let the sheriff's office know what you said."

"Yeah, tell them if they come by and I don't answer, to knock on the side window. I might hear that if I'm sleeping."

"Will do."

I watched her shuffle up her driveway and made sure she got inside before climbing in my car. As I did, Bud Crowder's garage door opened and he came out. I quickly closed my door, then watched as he opened his car trunk and pulled out a large duffle bag. It must have been heavy, because he struggled. When he got it on the ground, he shut the trunk and lifted the bag upright, pulled out a handle, and rolled it toward the garage.

I dialed Dylan's number, but it went to voicemail, so I sent a quick text asking him to call when he could because I had information.

Then I called Belle, who, thankfully, answered. "Bud Crowder bought a gun."

"Well butter my butt and call me a biscuit."

I couldn't help but laugh. "Right? This could be big. And there's rumors that Alice was having an affair with Roger Haines, the neighbor. You know, I may have just solved the case. Imagine how proud Dylan will be." I didn't believe that last part myself, but a girl could hope.

"Yes, that's exactly how Dylan will feel. How did you find all this out?"

"I talked to the neighbor across the street. Mayme Buckle or something like that. She also told me she heard the gunshot. Okay, she didn't say she heard it exactly, but she heard what she thought was a car engine backfiring around the time of the murder."

"Well look at you go, Veronica Mars. You're kicking butt and taking names."

"When I talked to Mr. Haines, he was pretty emotional about Alice's death. He said they had coffee all the time, and Buddy even mentioned Haines's dog being around a lot. I'm not an expert, but..." I turned left onto the main road and headed toward my former client's townhouse. My heart sank a little as I passed. So much senseless tragedy. "And Haines is a widower, so there's that."

"I don't want to burst your bubble or anything, and you've got a pretty big bubble going on right now, but I've got some private investigating skills too, and I found out something you might want to know."

"Please, burst my bubble."

"I guess your gut knew what it was feeling. I found another auto shop that had the Audi. It's in Cumming off Atlanta Highway."

"Really? That's amazing. Confusing, but amazing. What did they say?"

"The guy I talked to said he didn't do the paperwork, and the kid who did wasn't in, but he did say it was there for two days early last week. No work was done yet, but someone came and picked it up. He's going to get in touch with the kid, and I said I'd call back later. I didn't want to give my number."

"How'd you get the information?"

"Uh..." I could tell by her voice that she knew she'd been busted.

"You told him you were with the sheriff's office, didn't you?"

Belle stumbled over her words. "I...I just...oh, fine. I did. I didn't think he'd tell me anything otherwise."

I laughed, hard. "I love you."

"How could you not? You've dragged me into your illegal investigating addiction and now I'm trapped. If you're going to go down, at least you'll have me to hold onto on the way. Of course, we'll probably end up single the rest of our lives, but whatever. We can live together like Bonnie and Henrietta."

"Uh, no. I will not end up single the rest of my life, and we sure aren't like Bonnie and Henrietta."

Belle laughed. "Which reminds me, our intervention is in a few hours. I feel like we need to solidify Millie's plan."

"I think we just wing it."

"That'll go over well with them. We need to get the town to pray. It's our only hope."

"You are in a sassy mood today for sure."

"It's my new pretend private investigator attitude. You have to be tough when you're digging for clues."

"On that note, I'm at day care for Bo. I'm going to run him to the park right quick. Can you call everyone except the battling biddies and tell them to be at my place by five? We can figure out what to do then."

"On it."

Bo greeted me with a drool-smeared face and freshly clipped nails. I knew they were clipped because they didn't dig into my thigh when he pawed me. I'd lost several pairs of leggings from those nails.

"Hey, buddy!" I rubbed his head, dodging the drool spots best I could. "Looks like you had fun today."

Emma, the newest front desk clerk, laughed. "He sure did. He's got a new bestie. You should see them together. I posted some pictures on our Facebook page."

"Great, I'll check them out."

"Will our guy be back tomorrow?"

I smiled at Bo, who looked up at me with what I swear was a smile on his face. "You wanna come back tomorrow, big guy?"

He swept the floor with his tail.

I smiled at Emma. "That's a yes."

"Great. I've got him on the list."

We made a quick run to the dog park. I tried to take him a

couple times a week. Doggie day care had a big outdoor area, but every time I stalked the live video on their website, they were inside. Yes, the inside had an open section leading outside, but dog mom guilt was brutal. If I saw him out there, it probably wouldn't be as brutal.

The county finally finished their improvements to the entire park, including the dog area and the lacrosse fields. They added an additional concessions building and painted it red and cream, the color of the park district's teams. They extended the parking lot, which took a bit of green space away but was badly needed. So many kids from all over played lacrosse, so the lot was full most of the time.

In the dog park, they filled several soggy areas with more dirt so they wouldn't flood during our heavier rain seasons, which, as of late, was every season. They also fenced off a section for older dogs, and I knew several people who'd be thrilled with that.

Bo must have played hard—hence the matted, dried drool head—because he didn't run at the park. He sniffed. A lot. I called it the "wonderful tour of smells," and thanked God I didn't have a nose that intense.

I sat on a bench and piddled on my phone while he finished his tour, and I nearly jumped off the thing when someone tapped my shoulder from behind. "Dylan Roberts! You about scared the pants off me!"

He did that twitchy thing with his mouth he does when he's being adorable. "I'd like to see that."

I swatted his arm. "Hush. I'm a lady."

He sat next to me. "My lady, so I'm allowed to say those kinds of things."

"What're you doing here? Shouldn't you be investigating a case? And how did you know I was here anyway?"

"Came because you wanted to tell me something. I am investigating a case, but I needed some air, and I went to day care to get Bo for you, but Emma said you'd just left with him. Did I cover them all?"

I smiled. "Yes, thank you."

"So, what'd you do now?"

"What do you mean?" I tried for an innocent lash batting but didn't pull it off.

"You interview more people? Find a secret clue and decide to share it with me?"

"You know me so well, but no. That's not it."

"Great. It's worse, isn't it?"

"Define worse."

CHAPTER 9

"It isn't anything bad."

"You never do anything bad. Not intentionally."

I shifted sideways on the bench so I could face him. Bo must have spotted him because he came charging toward us full throttle. He skidded to a stop when Dylan told him to sit.

"Good boy." He rubbed Bo's head, then pulled his hand away and rubbed it on his pants. "Is that dried spit?"

"Yup."

"That's disgusting."

"He made a new bestie. Thank God humans don't slobber when they meet new friends."

"Stop stalling. Just let me have it."

I inhaled and then let the breath out slowly. "I happened to be driving by the Crowder house and I—"

"You happened to be driving by?"

"On my way to day care."

"Which is on the other side of town."

"I thought it was a short cut?"

He rolled his eyes. "Go on."

"So as I happened to be driving by the Crowder house, the

woman across the street was out getting her mail. By the way, I bet when she's mad, she could give Millie a run for her money."

He kept his lips in a thin, straight line.

"Okay, so she told me she might have heard the gunshot, but she didn't recognize it at the time because there's a kid down the street with a hot rod—her words, not mine—whose engine—"

"Backfires all the time. I already know this. And I'm pretty sure my guys talked to her already."

"No, they didn't. She took some sleeping pills, and if they did stop by, which I'm sure they did because your guys are awesome, she didn't hear the bell. In fact, she said next time y'all come by and she doesn't answer, to knock on the side window so she hears you."

He tipped his head down and shook it.

"Anyway, she said Bud Crowder came over with a new gun he bought. Said he showed it to her husband, but she didn't get a good look at it. She said it's not big like her husband's hunting rifles. She also said there's rumors that Alice was having an affair, and she thinks it's with the neighbor, Roger Haines, the one with the dog. Oh! And she saw the car leaving the house, Dylan. After she heard the loud bang. So did Roger Haines, by the way."

"You talked to him too?"

I cringed. "I thought I told you that."

"Nope."

"I didn't tell you about the first time?"

"First time?"

I cringed again.

"You might have. I've had so many people coming at me with stuff I need my white board to keep it all straight. Go on."

"Okay, so something about the car just doesn't sit right with me. I had this feeling, you know, women's intuition and all, that we needed to check other auto shops."

"We already know which auto shop it was at. Why would we have to check other shops?"

"That's the intuition part. It was just a feeling. Belle called the auto shops around the area and found one on Atlanta Highway in Cumming that had the car last week. The guy said it was there for two days and someone came and picked it up. I don't think the car was ever at the outlet mall."

He stared at me for a moment, probably letting it all sink in. I had a habit of talking at lightning speed when I got nervous or excited, and I was both at that moment. And maybe a little scared.

"So let me get this straight, Miss A Mile A Minute." He repeated back what I'd said, only using fewer words and a deeper voice.

"Yes, but I have two questions. If both Mayme whatever-her-last-name-is and Roger Haines saw the car leave after the shooting, who was driving? Also, why would someone at the outlet mall lie? Oh, the neighbor also said she goes out to get the mail when she hears the mail truck, and that's when she saw the car leave. I asked her what time that was, but all she said was the time it comes every day or something like that."

"You'd think a woman who could hear a mail truck could hear her doorbell."

"She took the pill after she got the mail."

"It's possible. I'll have my guys try and talk to her again."

"But you see it, right?"

"See what?"

"If Alice Crowder was having an affair, and her husband knew it, he could have bought the gun because of it, and they'd fought, so it's possible he killed her." I kicked a rock on the ground. "And that's why he was MIA for so long. It fits. I think he's the killer."

"We haven't cleared him as a suspect yet, but he told me

where he was, and we were able to verify it, at least to some degree."

"Where was he?"

"Hotel just outside of town. Said he went there because he was frustrated with his wife. They'd had an argument, and he needed to get away. Manager verified he stayed, just couldn't say if he was there during the time of the murder."

"He went to a hotel because of a fight over the dishes?"

"Everyone has their limits."

He wasn't just talking about Bud Crowder, was he? "Don't they have video cameras?"

"Most places have them, but they're just for show. Security services are expensive, and he stayed at a dump, so we didn't expect them to have one that worked."

"So he could have come back. I don't know, maybe he picked up his wife's car early without her knowing it so it would look like she drove it home. He goes in, kills her, then leaves in the car so if anyone's watching, they think it's her leaving. Clears him from the scene completely."

He smiled. "We're working a similar theory." He squeezed my leg. "I'm not going to be home until late, but I think there's a way you can help me. It'll have to be tomorrow, though, because of your intervention tonight."

"I'm so not looking forward to that."

"I don't want to be thankful for a murder investigation, but…"

I had to laugh, awful as it was.

"There's an auto theft ring in Atlanta that's branched out as far as Alpharetta. It's possible it's spreading farther north, and the Crowder car could be a part of that, or a separate issue entirely."

"If you're asking me to steal a car, um, no."

He chuckled. "The outlet mall is halfway between here and Alpharetta. We checked with the property management company and they said they didn't call in the vehicle."

"Interesting."

He nodded. "But they said all the store managers have the number for the towing company, and any of them could have made the call. I had them ask around, and the Burberry store manager called it in."

"And probably lied about it."

"That's what I'd like to find out. She could be a plant for the theft ring."

"Really? A woman?"

"You'd be surprised how many women are involved in that kind of thing. I'm not sure this is connected, and I'll be honest, I lean toward the husband for the murder, but it needs to be checked out."

"And you want me to talk to her?"

"If she's involved and we talk to her, she'll think we're onto her, and we can't have that. Not yet."

I pointed at my chest as my eyes grew the size of basketballs. "You want me to talk to a potential car thief?"

"I wouldn't send you somewhere I thought you'd be in danger."

"I'll do it."

"I never doubted you."

"I can go when the place opens tomorrow. My fee is a hundred dollars an hour."

"Right."

I leaned my head into the upper half of his arm. "Can I do that now instead of the intervention? I think it'll be a heck of a lot easier."

He laughed. "I'm not sure why you offered to do that anyway."

I sighed as I lifted my head. "It has to be done. You saw them when you kicked them out of Millie's. They left together. They're best friends, and they need each other. They just need a little push to remember that."

"It's their fight. Their business."

"It's impacting the entire town, Dylan. People are taking sides. Just the other day Billy Ray said the firemen had a poll about which one is scarier mad, and I heard someone bet twenty bucks on who would win in a battle."

The side of his mouth twitched. "Who won?"

"Bonnie, by a landslide."

He full-out laughed at that. "Yeah, I'd have picked her too. Woman's got a mouth like a truck driver."

I pushed my shoulder into his arm. "Don't be ugly. I'm worried about them."

"I know, and you know I support your effort to help." He shifted on the bench to face me. "Just be careful, okay? I don't need you getting caught in the crossfire and hurt by a cane or a walker or something."

I rolled my eyes. "They don't use canes or walkers."

"You never know what those two will bring to a battle."

He was right.

~

Bo was already snoozing in the back of my car when I pulled out of the park's lot. Two minutes later, as I passed the church, he was full-out snoring. Home was just a holler away, and I felt bad for waking him from his joyful exhaustion, so I drove around town a bit. I needed to do that anyway to scope out the competition.

Just last month a new realty agency set their sights on Bramblett County, filling the void left by our previous competition, a recently retired couple who hadn't done much in the market in years. The newbies had hit the road running, leaving flyers all over town—on car windows, in mailboxes, hanging in our few stores on Main Street. They also went door to door introducing themselves. The night they showed up at my door and gave me their sales pitch, I showed them a new flyer Belle designed with our "realtor of the year for the north Georgia area" star on it. They wiped the egg off their face and left.

Belle got a bug up her behind about it, and kicked up her marketing efforts by a thousand percent. Main Street had exactly ten benches lining each side of the square, and our faces—including Bo's—were on every single one of them. Our business was the first billboard off the expressway toward town, again with our faces—including Bo's—showing our pearly whites for the world to see. Our part of the world, anyway. She hit the surrounding towns, too. Even Castleberry had benches with our faces on them. Bonnie said we were floozies seen all over town, and in a way, she was right.

Belle upped our marketing in other ways too, getting us more involved in town events because, according to her, the six events we already sponsored and volunteered for weren't enough. Her efforts worked. We saw a fifteen-percent increase in our listings outside of town, many of them in Castleberry. Apparently having your face staring out at the town worked.

I drove out to the mixed-use development on the outskirts of town, saying a little prayer as I passed by. I often wondered how Myrtle Redbecker would feel about her property. Her neighbors ended up selling too, something most of Bramblett considered a miracle. Money talked, and when it had a lot to say, people usually listened. The development expanded, and continued to grow. I'd lost two people there, and for a while I wondered if I was the problem, if I had a curse attached to me. Both Belle and Dylan convinced me otherwise, so I tucked the thought in the back of my mind, but every now and again it crept out to remind me it still had meaning.

Bo snored so loudly he woke himself up. We were just a few houses from home. He crawled into the passenger seat and stared at me, drool dripping from the side of his mouth.

"Ew. Come on, not in my car. I just cleaned it."

The rebel in him didn't seem to care, and he shook his head

back and forth. Spit flew through my car, hitting the back seat, dashboard, and front window.

"Bo Sprayberry Roberts! That's disgusting."

He barked.

"Don't you sass me, mister."

He barked again, and I realized he was barking at the car in our driveway. It was Belle's. Bo knew her car, and every time she came over, he was like a puppy, full of excitement and energy, even if he was exhausted. Who was I kidding, he was like that any time anyone came over.

"It's Auntie Belle! You make sure to go in and give her a big, wet smooch, okay?"

He barked again.

I swore the dog spoke English.

Belle opened the door, and Bo charged her. As I got my things out of my car I heard her grunting and laughing, and a few no's and ew's too. Bo may have lived with just two people, but his family was big, and he was everyone's favorite.

Belle dragged her hands down her jeans. "Got my puppy bath for the day."

"He loves you."

"If only Matthew showered me with that kind of affection."

"Right?"

"So, have you figured out what we're going to do yet?"

"I was kind of hoping Millie would come up with something."

She poured herself a glass of wine. "I brought this just in case. I should have brought two."

Billy Ray and Old Man Goodson knocked on the door.

"It's open," I hollered. I fixed Bo his dinner and set it on the floor next to a fresh bowl of water.

Billy Ray walked in dressed for... I didn't know what.

Belle eyed him, her right brow pushing toward her hairline. "What in the devil are you wearing?"

"I'm protecting myself."

She held back a laugh. "From what? A nuclear bomb?"

That seemed about right. He'd layered up in two sweaters, a button down, a pair of gloves, and a pair of jeans. Either he had leg muscles we'd never seen, or he wore something under those jeans, because they were tight and poufy. He walked funny, too, like he couldn't bend his knees.

"I got me on my defensive gear. I got scratches and bruises on my arms from being dragged around by them ladies. I'm on the blood thinners, and I don't want to bleed out and die on your floor." He pushed up the three layers on his arm. "Lookie here. It's still bleeding."

Belle chuckled. "I promise we'll keep you safe. You will not die on the floor."

"Oh my, let me see that." I held his arm carefully.

Billy Ray wasn't a young whipper-snapper anymore. Those days had long passed. But the blood bruises and age spots on his arm surprised me anyway. I realized these people I'd grown to consider family, people who'd been there for me and were willing to risk their lives for me, wouldn't be around forever. And their time could be short, too. I wiped the blood from his arm, patted it clean with hydrogen peroxide, then swiped a bit of Neosporin over it and gently placed two band-aids on the cut to make sure the blood didn't soak through.

Belle poured him a glass of sweet iced tea. "Here, I'm told by a very credible source this and a band-aid are a cure-all for whatever ails you." She smiled and winked at him.

He smiled at Belle. "You don't know these ladies. Bonnie ain't had one of them mani-pedi things in weeks. Said she can't go back to that place 'cause of the memories. And her nails? They're like knives."

Ouch.

"What memories?" Belle asked.

"Heck if I know. I just listen. I ain't stupid enough to talk. Not while they're pitching fits anyway."

Old Man Goodson nodded. "Our lives are at risk, least till they make up. What's the plan for this thing anyway? I got the VCR set to record *Law & Order*, but I'd like to be home in time to watch it."

"We'll do our best," I said, and offered him something to drink.

As we sat down to formulate a plan, Millie rapped on the door. She didn't wait for anyone to answer.

Once inside, she set a box of things on the table. "Okay, I got us a plan." She detailed it out and we all got to doing what she asked, writing words on our individual index cards.

"We're going to get these two back on track or die trying," Millie said.

I had a feeling we'd all die trying.

CHAPTER 10

Millie's plan was good to go. After we finished writing out the last of our cards, she took them all and read them, chuckling at a few and laughing hard at others, then plopped them into the boxes. She'd barely finished when Bonnie knocked on the door.

Belle got Bonnie and the rest of the crew situated in my small family room while I finished preparing a few plates of snacks. Pimento cheese with crackers, a traditional southern favorite, potato chips with ranch dip, and a small bowl of baby carrots as well as some little tomatoes and olives.

Henrietta showed up, scowl plastered on her face, her hair up in curlers. She wasn't happy at all.

I gave her a hug. "I see you dressed for the occasion."

"I wash my hair this night every week. Don't plan on changing that because of that old biddy."

"Come on now. At least try to be kind."

She grumbled something I didn't understand. We walked into the family room, and Belle sat her on the opposite side of the coffee table as far as she could get from Bonnie while still being in the same room.

Smart move, I thought.

Millie had the table cleared and three boxes set up on it. I let her take charge. She was good at that.

She stood in front of us, her eyes traveling between Bonnie and Henrietta. "Now, I know you two don't want to keep this up, and none of us are interested in dealing with your hissy fits anymore either—"

Bonnie huffed, and Henrietta said, "I'm not the one pitching a fit. Don't be—"

"Shut your trap, woman. We're fixin' this tonight whether you like it or not, you hear?"

Go Millie. She definitely had a career in divorce mediation if she wanted.

Millie was holding a box tight against her chest. She hadn't let any of us see which cards were in which box, but we didn't care. We just wanted it all done so we could go to sleep. I, for one, was exhausted, and the smell of those olives made me feel icky.

"So here's what we're going to do." She pointed to the boxes. "Each of those boxes has index cards in them. On each card is a word. All of us here, all of us who care about you, we wrote words we feel describe you—all the good things, that is. In this box are the ones for Bonnie." She pointed to the other box. "And this one's Henrietta's."

"What's in the one you're holding?" Bonnie asked. "Our bad stuff?"

Belle pressed her lips together. I stopped looking at her for fear she'd make me laugh. It might have been funny, but their fight was serious, and we needed to help reunite them, fix what was broken.

"You just fall off the turnip truck, woman? This isn't a negativity game, it's a positive one. In that box are things about your friendship, good things."

Bonnie leaned toward a box and tried to peek inside, but Millie stopped her.

"Eh, nope. You don't get to look. Here's what we're going to do. You each get a turn picking one card from the other person's box. You read the word out loud, and you tell us how it applies to her. No negative nelly stuff either, you hear?"

Millie's idea was sheer brilliance, and I stored it in the back of my brain for the future, like when Dylan and I had a house full of kids battling each other daily.

Bonnie nearly choked on her words. "You mean I gotta say something nice about that who's-a-what? There ain't nothing nice to say about her."

Belle skirted over to Henrietta and wrapped her arm around her.

Millie pointed at Bonnie. "Okay, Ms. Happy Pants, you go first."

Bonnie grunted. She refused to pick a card from the box, so Old Man Goodson took one and handed it to her.

"I don't wanna."

"Don't matter. Those are the rules," he said.

"She ain't the boss of me. I don't have to do what she says."

Old Man Goodson's face reddened quickly. "Darn you, woman, you're going to do this whether you like it or not. Me and Billy Ray here, we're tired of being pulled into your…your ugliness. Why, we're about ready to trade you two in for younger models, you hear me?"

Belle's chin dropped. Mine did too. Even Bo, who'd been snoring away on his bed beside the couch, looked up and groaned. Old Man Goodson had guts. Good for him.

Bonnie yanked the card from his hand. "You egg-sucking dog. No more back rubs for you."

Belle cringed and mouthed "TMI" to me. I nodded my agreement.

Bonnie read the card to herself and then shook her head. "For crying out loud, this ain't gonna work."

Millie kept her face emotionless. "Read it." The woman should have been an elementary school lunch lady.

She growled it out, her eyes narrowed and aimed at her feet. "Unobtrusive."

"Okay, good. Now, how does that relate to Henrietta? Use it in a sentence to describe her."

She groaned.

Millie huffed. "You need me to tell you what it means?"

Bonnie narrowed her eyes at her. "I didn't just fall off the turnip truck. I had me an education." She read the card out loud, though her tone made it obvious she didn't want to. "Henrietta is as unobtrusive as a bull in a china shop."

Belle laughed and Millie shot daggers at her. She ran her finger across her lip, promising to zip it.

"Try again," Millie said. "And remember, keep it positive."

Bonnie scrunched her eyes and stared at Millie, then let that stare hit each of us, finally landing on Henrietta. "Henrietta ain't all unobtrusive sometimes. Most of the time, but not all the time."

Millie dug into the box she held, removed something, and tossed it at Bonnie, whacking her in the head with it. "Nope. Try again."

The thing, a small piece of green spongy material, landed on my floor.

Bonnie eyed it, then whipped her head toward Millie. "That hurt!"

Millie waved it off. "It's a piece of a Nerf ball. It couldn't hurt a flea." She glanced at Henrietta. "Each time y'all say something negative, I got something in this box, and I'm gonna whip it at you. The sooner you get serious, the sooner we can all go home. Now come on, get to it." She eyed Bonnie sternly.

"I thought you said there were positive things about our friendship in that box?" Henrietta asked.

"I lied." She eyed Bonnie again. "Go on now."

"Fine." She picked up the Nerf scrap and set it on the table. "Henrietta's more fun when she's obtrusive, not unobtrusive."

Nobody moved for a moment. I think we were all afraid of lightning striking or pigs flying into the windows. It wasn't a glowing reference for her best friend, but it was something.

Finally, Millie smiled. "That's a start." She held the other box toward Henrietta. "Your turn."

Henrietta dug into the box and pulled out a card. She read it, raised her eyebrow, and leaned back, shaking her head. "Nope. I'm not saying this one. It's not right."

"Read it."

She shook her head.

Belle placed her hand on Henrietta's knee. "Come on, you can do it."

Henrietta read the card again and grimaced. "I got to use it in a sentence?"

Millie nodded.

"And you're sure it's got to be positive?"

"Yes, Henrietta. Now come on, get on with it."

She huffed loudly. "Billy Ray and Old Man Goodson think Bonnie is sexy, but they know I'm sexier."

I turned my head toward the wall. I could not look at Belle. I knew if I did, I'd bust out laughing. But it didn't matter. We were best friends, and best friends knew what the other was thinking without even looking. They knew their every expression, the glint in their eye, the slightly open mouth...they knew what it all meant. And I knew Belle was flat-out dying sitting next to Henrietta. I couldn't help it. I covered my mouth, and I tried, I really did, but the burst of laughter escaped anyway, and it started a trickle of other laughs, including from Bonnie and Henrietta.

Everyone laughed so hard we had tears in our eyes. Finally, Millie blew a whistle she had attached to a lanyard around her neck. I had no idea she'd brought it, but when she blew it, Bo sprang off the floor and all but hit the ceiling. He took off running, searching for somewhere his ears would be protected from the high-pitched sound.

"Okay, now that y'all had your laughs, let's get back to it." She pointed at Old Man Goodson and Billy Ray. "I told you two no funny stuff."

"You checked our cards. We didn't write it," Billy Ray said.

I glanced at Old Man Goodson, who winked at me and whispered, "I saved me an extra card and tossed it in there when she wasn't looking."

I wiggled my finger at him, but the smile taking over my face showed my real feelings. I loved me some Old Man Goodson. There was so much to him, so much most people didn't know, and I'd been lucky to gain his trust enough to be able to learn the wonderful secrets about him.

Millie's patience was waning, so she plucked a card from the box and handed it to Henrietta, but not before reading it herself first. "Here."

Henrietta read the word and kept her head down, staring at the card. I could have been wrong, but I thought she was honestly considering the word carefully.

"Go on now, read it. You want to get home and get those things out of your hair, don't you?"

"I do that tomorrow."

My mother used to use those prickly curlers. She'd wrap her hair in them in three sections, the top rolled back and the sides rolled down. Then she'd wrap an extra-thick pink cotton towel around them and hold it together with a clip. Sometimes she'd drive me to school with those things in her hair and I was horrified. She said if it was good enough for her momma, it was good enough for my momma. What always confused me was she had a curling iron, but she hated to use it; it would be a cold day in Hades, she'd said, when she'd let me curl her hair with that thing.

I gave Henrietta a lot of credit for sleeping on plastic knives like that.

"Then hurry it up. Some of us want to get some sleep before the sun comes up."

Henrietta let out a long breath and then said, "Clean. Bonnie likes her house to stay clean."

"Darn right I do."

Millie waved her hand at Bonnie. "Hush." And then she smiled at Henrietta. "That's excellent. I'm proud of you."

Bonnie wasn't going to let her temporary archnemesis steal her thunder, nor would she let her say something nice about her without topping it. She yanked the other box toward her and snatched a card from it. "Funny." She tilted her chin up and shook her head, then, after a moment, said, "When I'm sad, Henrietta says something funny to cheer me up."

Old Man Goodson and Billy Ray shifted their eyes to each other. Old Man Goodson raised his eyebrows. We were finally getting somewhere. I hoped.

"Good job, Bonnie. See, I knew you could do this."

"I can do better than that," Henrietta said. She scooted to the edge of the chair and put the box on her lap. Before Millie could tell her otherwise, she had two index cards in her hand, and she'd shoved the box onto Belle's lap.

Oh boy, I thought. It might not have been progress like I thought, but more competition instead.

"Only one," Millie said.

Henrietta's eyes popped. "But I got me two. I can't put one back, you're never allowed to put a card back in other games. You got to keep it."

Millie groaned and flicked her hand at the woman. "Fine. Go on."

She pushed herself off the chair and stood, holding both cards. "Honest and compassionate. Those are my words." She tapped her finger to her chin. "Let's see. Oh! Bonnie was compassionate to let me stay with her." She tilted her head. "Is that the right way to use the word?"

Millie nodded.

"Good, 'cause I don't profess to have perfect grammar or nothing like that."

She wasn't lying.

She held the second card up to her face to read it, and then dropped her hand to her side. "Honest. Bonnie might have been honest about me being a pain in the butt to live with, but I'm an old woman. I'm set in my ways. I didn't mean nothing by it. And I even offered to buy her a new tube of toothpaste. Matter of fact, I asked Old Man Goodson to take me to the Costco so I could get her one of those multi-packs. Didn't I?"

Old Man Goodson nodded. "Yes, she did. We were planning on going, but then the fight happened, and she changed her mind."

Was that just an apology on her part?

Bonnie's bottom lip quivered. "What kind were you getting?"

Henrietta shrugged. "Never know what you'll get at the Costco."

Millie broke in. "Now Bonnie, that was nice of Henrietta, wasn't it?"

Bonnie grumbled, but admitted that yes, it was nice.

"Now go on, pick a card. It's your turn."

Bonnie shoved her hand into the box and pulled out a card. "Dagnabbit. I don't want to do this anymore. It won't help. All she's got to do is say she's sorry. I'd even consider letting her stay with me again if she said it and promised not to throw her laundry all over the bathroom. I slipped on her...her..." She looked straight into Henrietta's eyes and said, "Over-the-shoulder boulder holder, and I almost broke my butt." She rubbed her backside. "Still got me the bruise too. Wanna see?"

She began lifting her potato-sack-style blue and white dress, but I stopped her as quickly as possible. "No, no. It's okay. We believe you, Bonnie."

Billy Ray chuckled.

Henrietta threw her hands in the air. "What do I got to say I'm sorry for? You told me your house was my house, and at my house, I leave my dirty clothes on the bathroom floor. I did what you said, then you turned around and changed your mind. What am I supposed to do?"

Well, darn.

"I think you both need to apologize to each other," I said, standing to make my point. "When I was thirteen, I had a birthday party."

"You're seriously bringing this up?" Belle asked.

I held up my finger. "My momma set it all up in our backyard, and she got one of those big blowup waterslides that went into the pool. This was before my brother crashed his four-wheeler into the pool and tore it to bits."

"I remember that," Billy Ray said. "Fire department came out because he hit that big tree in your parents' yard. Thought he had himself a concussion."

"Yes, right. So, I had, I don't know, fifteen kids at the party, Belle included, of course."

"Of course," Millie said.

"But, and I don't remember the reason exactly—"

Belle raised her hand. "I do. You wanted to go on family vacation with her."

"Right. Okay, so at the party, I paid the most attention to Heather."

Bonnie said, "God rest her soul," and made the sign of the cross across her chest.

"God rest her soul. Anyway, Belle's right. Heather's parents were going to Florida over summer break, and they told her she could invite one friend for a week. All of us"—I pointed at Belle—"wanted to go. To make my desire known,

I kind of picked her for everything at my party. She got to go down the slide with me first, she got to eat the second piece of cake, and she got to sleep over. Among other things."

"Yeah, many other things," Belle said.

"I didn't do it intentionally to hurt anyone. I just really wanted to go to Florida. But, the thing is, I did hurt someone. I hurt my best friend." I bent my head and shrugged. "It took me a while to realize, and when I did, I was mad at her for being mad at me because I was embarrassed about how I behaved."

"What's this got to do with us? I don't even have a pool," Bonnie said.

"No, but you have a best friend, and you both hurt each other, and you're both acting like teenage girls."

Billy Ray almost choked on his sweet tea.

"She started it." Henrietta pointed a long, skinny finger at Bonnie.

"Come on, ladies, the point is, you two are best friends, and you're fighting over something that my momma would say couldn't hold up a flea—" I shook my head. "Or something like that."

"She's not my friend," Henrietta said. "She kicked me out of her house for nothing. Heck, I wouldn't get out of the electric chair to go to her funeral." She grabbed her bag and headed toward the kitchen. "And another thing. She wears granny panties."

Belle bit her lip.

Bonnie rushed toward her. "You and I won't never be friends, you hear me?" She sniffled. "Never."

Henrietta opened the kitchen door, hollered, "Fine by me," and charged out.

Bonnie picked up her purse. "You think we're gonna kiss and make up? You all got another thing coming." She stormed out right behind her former best friend.

"Well," Old Man Goodson said. "That went just about how I thought it would."

I fell back into my chair and groaned.

~

Belle stuck around and helped me clean up. She plucked a carrot from the bowl and popped it in her mouth. Not bothering with proper manners, she said, "Bramblett as we know it is gone forever."

"We're screwed."

"Right?"

"We need to find a way to bring them together, you know? Something that'll force them to work together or something."

"Honey, you're going to need a miracle for that."

She'd poured herself another glass, and I took it from her and sipped it. "I know."

My cell phone rang, and I checked the caller ID. It was Matthew. I clicked the speaker button. "You looking for your significant other?"

"Dylan asked me to give you a quick call."

My eyes widened. "Is he okay?"

"He's fine. He's arresting Bud Crowder."

"And he wanted me to know?"

"Thought you might want to check on the son."

"Oh, got it. Is he charging him with murder?"

"Not yet. His neighbor caught him tossing a brick into his window. They had a little confrontation, and the neighbor's pressing charges."

Belle said hi and goodbye, and we hung up. She yawned and stretched. "I'm out of here. Sleep calls, and I'm answering. See you at Millie's in the morning?"

"Yeah, and then I've got to go to the outlet mall, so I'll be late to the office."

"Gotcha." She hugged me and left.

Bo was already on our bed, snuggled up on top of our pillows. Dylan hated that, but I didn't mind. I sent a quick text to Buddy Crowder to check on him. He responded a few minutes later with a quick, impersonal response.

Thoughts raced through my mind. Thoughts about Henrietta and Bonnie, Alice Crowder, and even that stupid fight at my birthday party. At some point I dozed off, and I didn't even wake up when Dylan crawled into bed.

CHAPTER 11

*N*either Bonnie nor Henrietta showed up at Millie's the next morning. Belle and I considered checking on them, but Millie assured us Henrietta was on her couch watching game shows. She'd said she'd come by the café later, after that floozy in the ugly dresses left.

The funny thing was, they traded dresses often.

Belle stirred a packet of stevia into her latte. "Any news on the big arrest last night?"

I shook my head. "Dylan got in late and was up and gone when I got up this morning."

"Poor guy."

"Yeah, he's probably exhausted. I'm heading to the outlet mall in a bit, and then I'll probably run by the station to tell him what I got, if I get anything."

"No problemo. I've got two appointments today in Castleberry. Two potential clients."

"That's awesome. You're the marketing queen."

She leaned back in her chair. "Nah, it's our faces. They look great on the benches."

"Yeah, it's got nothing to do with our reputation. It's all about our looks."

"Duh. I mean, who wouldn't want to list their home with two beauties like us?"

I squinted at her face.

"What?" She touched her chin. "Do I have something on my face?"

I squinted harder. "I think it's a black chin hair."

She pushed her head back and rubbed her fingers all over her chin. "Where?"

I pressed my lips together and raised my eyebrows.

"You are an awful person."

"I know." I sipped my hot tea. "And it's awesome." I gathered my things. "I've got to go. I want to get to the mall right when it opens, and then, if you don't mind, I'm going to see a man about an arrest."

"Your husband?"

"Well, him too, but I meant the man who's pressing charges. Roger Haines."

"Oh. Have fun with that, Veronica."

"Stop calling me that. She's a high schooler."

"Yeah, but she plays pretend private eye just like you."

"Love you too," I said as I let the door close behind me.

～

Dylan told me the store manager called the tow company because a car had been parked in her regular spot for several days. He was able to get her name and a description of her car so I could see if it was in the spot she claimed was her regular one. I drove to the spot–at least I was pretty sure it was the spot—and backed in next to it. I got out of my car and pretended to get something from my trunk, but really just took photos of the license plate to send to Dylan. I didn't know if he needed them, but I felt a sense of pride in doing so.

The mall just opened, so I headed straight for the store, though I had no idea if she was working. The outlet mall traffic didn't pick up until just before lunch time, so the odds of her being there were slim, but I'd go back later if necessary.

I pretended to shop and found two things I liked, but even for an outlet store, the prices were well above my budget. Who spent two hundred dollars on a wool scarf? Better yet, who would pay the three hundred it cost originally? I couldn't fathom spending that kind of money on a foot of wool, no matter how much I loved the plaid pattern.

A tall woman in gray slacks and a white top stepped out from the back room. "Can I help you find anything today?"

She stumped me right then. It was her, and I wanted to talk to her, but how did I even start the conversation?

"That's a beautiful scarf. We have it in gray also." She walked over to another scarf and wrapped it around her neck. "I'm partial to the gray, but—" She glanced down at her pants. "That's obvious, I guess." She took the scarf and wrapped it around my neck, turning me toward the full-length mirror on the wall.

I almost drooled. And I totally understood why people spent that kind of money on a scarf.

"It's lovely with your eyes, and it's got class written all over it, don't you think?"

"Yes, it does. But I think I need something a little longer, maybe thinner? I'm going away for the weekend with my husband, and we're taking his car. He's got an Audi convertible. Tiny little thing, really, and my hair just blows all over." I let my southern accent shine. Lying didn't count if it was done to solve a crime. I tried hard to convince myself of that.

"Oh, I love those little cars. You've got the perfect head for this, though, but I get your point. Hold on, I think I've got something over here." She walked over to a small table with different items spread across it. "Yup, here it is. The last one. I love this scarf." She held up another gray one, longer and thinner than the wool one. "It's a mix of silk and wool. Here, feel it. It's perfect for a convertible ride."

I rubbed the soft, silky, heavenly material. "Oh, that is nice."

She wrapped it over my head, flipping one end under my chin and over my shoulder. "Look at you, all sexy and ready for a convertible ride!"

She had me convinced. If I had the cash on hand to blow on a scarf, I would have, right then and there. The woman knew how to work a sale. "Do you have any gloves? I would just love a set to go with my scarf. My hands might get chilly for the ride."

She led me to a basket with various sets of gloves tucked around the rim. When she handed me a pair that cost seventy-five bucks, I wondered if that was the low end of the basket. I slipped them on. "These are gorgeous."

"Yes they are, and they look perfect with the scarf. Oh, I have this sweater, it's to die for, and would be stunning on you!" She walked over to a section of hanging clothes and searched the rack. When she pulled out the sweater, I wanted to grab it and run. "Isn't it beautiful?"

"Yes, it is." I needed an in. I thought mentioning the Audi was my in, but she distracted me with my dream scarf, and the gloves really messed up my plan, not to mention the sweater. Dear Jesus, the sweater. Without considering the consequences, I just blurted out, "Did you hear about that woman they found dead in her house? Awful, isn't it?"

"It's horrible." She glanced around the store and whispered, "And I found the woman's car too. I don't want anyone to know, though. I don't want to get involved in a murder. You never know what the killer would do to me if he found out."

"Oh, I understand. I would never be involved in any murder investigation. It's too dangerous. I think that's incredible that you found her car. I didn't know it was missing, though. What happened?"

She nodded. "Someone just dumped it in my regular spot here. Can you believe that? What are the odds? I have a connection at the sheriff's, and it was in my spot for five days. You know, just sitting there. So, I called and had it towed. I didn't find out until the other day it was connected to the murder."

"Wow, that's amazing."

"Yeah, I mean, what if it was some random thing, and the killer found her here, abducted her, then made her go to her house to rob it, and he just killed her there? It could have been me."

"Right? How awful. You are so lucky. And it was there five days? I'm surprised you didn't report it sooner."

We walked toward the counter. "Honestly, it could have been longer. I was off Sunday and Monday."

"I didn't hear about the car. I guess I should pay more attention, shouldn't I?"

She fidgeted with the sweater, rubbing the soft wool against her hands, and then set it on the counter and picked up the scarf. "So, scarf and gloves? What about the sweater?"

"Oh, I uh…" I pushed the scarf and sweater aside. "Just the gloves. I'm on a budget." I'd have to sneak back to return them when she wasn't working.

"Sure, I get it. I can't afford half this stuff anyway. Thank God for employee discounts."

She wrapped my unnecessary purchase in tissue paper, taped it, and then gently placed it in a bag. At what it cost, it deserved to be treated with gentle hands.

I learned a few things from the manager. Most importantly, she gave me a different timeframe about when she first saw the car, and when she called to have it towed, and she completely blabbed about something that hadn't been made public. Either she wasn't involved in the car theft ring Dylan mentioned or she wasn't that smart. I couldn't decide which, but I'd done what Dylan asked, and I couldn't wait to tell him. I dialed his number but, as usual, got his voicemail and left a message.

A crowd gathered in front of our office and stretched the few doors down to Millie's, blocking three parking spaces facing the building.

"What the heck?"

I passed the group, looped back around, and parked directly across from my office. It didn't take long to push through the crowd and see what the commotion was about.

"That Henrietta floozy got me kicked out. The sheriff won't even let me have my morning coffee." Bonnie held a poster board sign that read *Kisses for Coffee*. I read it twice to make sure I didn't get it wrong, and each time it said the same thing. I shook my head, half humored and half annoyed at her effort to cause a scene.

Belle pushed up beside me. "Did you see the other one?"

I raised my eyebrows. "Please, no."

"Oh, it's good." She grabbed a hold of my arm and shoved through the small crowd. "'Scuse me. Coming through."

"Tongue kisses for tea? Oh. My. Goodness."

Belle laughed. "Right? If I had to choose, I'd get her the coffee."

Two teenage boys shoved their way in front of us. One hooted, and the other hollered, "Oh yeah! That's what I'm talking about."

I grabbed the yeller—Jacob Rush, whose mother worked on the Christmas festival committee with me—by the shoulder and squeezed tighter than I probably should, forcing him to face me. "Your momma finds out you're talking like that to a lady and she'll have you get two switches from that big oak tree in your backyard."

His eyes popped.

"I have her number in my cell. Should I give her a call?"

He dropped his head. "No, ma'am."

"Good. Now shouldn't you be at school?"

"Early release day, ma'am."

Did the county ever have full school days anymore? "Well, go on then, get out of here and I won't tell your momma."

"Yes, ma'am."

I gripped Belle's arm. "We have to do something."

Belle shrugged. "Last I checked, free speech was still a thing."

"I think this is more than free speech."

"I know. That's what makes it hilarious. How many women that age do you see soliciting on the side of the street?" She laughed. "This is better than people watching at the Walmart."

A loud bull horn behind us got everyone's attention.

Belle jumped on her tiptoes. "Look! That's my guy!"

Matthew spoke into the horn. "Move on, everyone. You're creating a fire hazard. Don't need the fire department coming out here and spraying y'all, now do we?"

Someone yelled from the crowd, "The *Gazette* needs pictures of this!"

"Already got 'em," another man hollered.

"Let's make it go viral," someone else hollered.

I sighed. "Great. These women are going to be the laughing-stock of town and the internet."

"I'm thinking they've pretty much been that for a while now in town," Belle said. "The internet, though, that'll be something."

After Matthew encouraged people to leave with passive threats of tickets, the crowd finally dispersed. Bonnie and Henrietta stayed on their respective sides of the stores holding their signs, proud as pigs in mud.

Matthew removed his hat, rubbed the top of his head, and then put it on again.

"He doesn't look pleased," I whispered.

He walked over to us and gave a slight nod. "Ladies."

Bonnie held her sign proudly in front of her chest. Matthew read it and shook his head. He turned toward Henrietta, read her sign, then bent his head and shook it. "I should have stayed in Atlanta. The prostitutes were easier to deal with there."

Henrietta's eyes widened. "I ain't no prostitute."

"She ain't sexy enough to be one of those," Bonnie said.

Belle and I moved between the women just in case purses started flying again.

Matthew placed his hands on his hips. "Ladies, you're offering sex for payment. That's called prostitution, and it's a felony with up to three years in prison in the state of Georgia."

"We aren't asking for money. We're asking for coffee," Bonnie said. She moved closer to Henrietta.

It amazed me that they could bond together for a cause without even realizing it, yet they couldn't acknowledge what they meant to each other.

"Yeah, and it's that sheriff's fault. We could get our own if he hadn't kicked us out of Millie's. We don't like the coffee at the drugstore," Henrietta said.

"Coffee, cash, it's the same thing when you're offering sex for it."

Bonnie let the sign drop to the ground. "I ain't offering sex. I'm like the kissing booth at the festival. They're not prostitutes, right? Otherwise you got to arrest your girl there, 'cause she was charging a dollar a kiss last time."

"Yeah, and I heard she didn't even use her tongue," Henrietta said.

Belle busted out laughing. "Okay, ladies, that's enough. Seriously, if you wanted a cup of coffee, all you had to do was ask someone to get it for you, or better yet, stop this silly fighting and act like adults."

"We are acting like adults," Henrietta said. "We could have worked this out days ago but all y'all had to stick your noses in our business and make things worse."

My mood shifted from happy to aggravated in a flash. Blaming us for their stubbornness? I had a mind to tell her what I thought about that, but it would have been ugly.

Matthew worked hard not to smile. At least someone thought they were funny, because I sure didn't. "Belle, can you get them each a cup of coffee, please? On the sheriff's office tab." He took Bonnie's sign first, then laughed as he took Henrietta's. "Did you find this on the internet or something?"

"Find what?"

I bit my lip.

"Never mind." He handed me the signs, giving me a little head shake in the process. "Would you put these in my cruiser, please? Passenger door's unlocked." He resumed his law enforcement officer stance, hands on hips, legs slightly spread. "Okay, here's what we're going to do."

Belle came out and handed each lady a coffee.

"We're going to get in my cruiser, and I'm going to take you down to the jail."

Bonnie gasped. "Are you arresting us?"

Henrietta's jaw shook. "I can't go to jail. I'm claustrophobic."

"You should have thought about that before you propositioned half the town." He angled to the side. "Now come on. I don't want to cuff you, but I will if I have to."

Belle and I were in shock. Was he kidding? Was he just going to bring them to the station and scare them, or did he actually plan to arrest them? I thought the idea was kind of brilliant, but I felt awful for thinking that. I nudged Belle with my arm. "Do something."

"Like what?"

"Tell him to stop."

"Honey, how many times have you tried that on Dylan when he's working?"

I winced. "Good point, but we have to do something."

"Fine." She walked over to her boyfriend and laid her southern belle accent on thick. "Matthew, sweetie, you're not going to arrest them, now are you?" She batted her eyelashes at him.

It didn't work. "Yes, ma'am. Like I said, prostitution's a felony." He opened the back door to his car and helped each one in. "Seat belts, please. It's the law, and we don't need you two breaking another one."

He smiled as he closed the door.

Belle stomped her foot. "Matthew Riley! You can't be serious!"

A smile stretched across his face, and he pulled Belle and me away from the car. "I'm not going to arrest them, but I am going to have a little fun with them."

"Is what they did really a felony?" I asked.

Matthew smirked. "Technically speaking, no. They weren't asking for cash, but it'd be up to a judge to decide if they should be punished."

"I don't think any judge would give jail time to two old ladies who wanted a cup of coffee," Belle said.

"You'd be surprised." He spoke into the radio on his shoulder. "This is Deputy Riley. I've got a ten-twenty-uh-something coming in. Two suspects. No priors. No outstanding warrants."

A woman spoke through his radio. "Deputy Riley, can you repeat the call?"

"Let's just say I've got possible public disturbance, and my unsubs need a place to cool off. Together."

The woman on the other end of the radio sounded confused. "Uh, yes, sir. Holding cell is available."

"Ten-four."

"What are you going to do?" I asked.

"Tell them I'm keeping them there till they work out their differences."

Belle chuckled. "Awesome!"

"Goodness, this could be bad."

Belle smirked. "Funny overrides bad in this case."

"Hey, Matthew, is Dylan in his office? I called but it went straight to voicemail."

"He's working on the white board for the Crowder case. Want me to give him a message?"

"Yes, please. Can you tell him I talked to the woman at the store? She kind of contradicted herself, and I wanted to tell him what she said."

"You mean the woman at Burberry? We already cleared that yesterday morning. Don't think she's involved."

My jaw tightened. "Oh, well, okay. I just thought I'd let him know."

He gave Belle a quick kiss and drove the women to the jail.

"Want a coffee?" Belle laughed. "But I'm not going to offer sex for one, just so you know."

"You know what? I think I'm good. I've got some work to do, but I think I'll work from home if you don't mind."

She tilted her head. "You okay?"

I wasn't, but I wasn't ready to talk about it, either. "Yeah, sure."

"Okay, I know you're lying like a dog on a rug, but you'll tell me when you're ready."

I nodded, not really paying attention to what she said. I was too wrapped up in the fact that my husband sent me on a wild goose chase for information he didn't actually need.

$\mathcal{M}$arriage is hard. My momma always says it takes compromise and effort, especially through the rough times. Dylan and I hadn't had rough times yet, at least not in our marriage. Sure, we'd struggled while dating, but the parameters are different, as are the rules. Marriage brought a whole new level to the game, and I had absolutely no experience in it.

I tried to work, even made a few client calls, but my mind kept returning to the thought that Dylan set me up to do something he knew was irrelevant.

Why would he do that? Was he trying to make me feel involved? To distract me so I wouldn't pursue my own investigation? I'd solved a few murders before he did. It wasn't a secret. Did that bother him? Did he worry about my safety, or was it just his ego? And most importantly, did any of it matter?

Considering the fact that I couldn't let it go, it obviously mattered to me.

When I needed a clear perspective, I did what any smart woman did. I called my mom.

"Lily! I was just going to call you! Did you hear what those silly old women did today? I got a call from Sally. You know, the lady who cut your hair when you were four and about sent your dad to the hospital because he thought you looked like a boy?"

My momma got Bramblett County's gossip faster than a hunting dog got its deer.

"Yes, I remember that well. I didn't grow my hair long again until college. And yes, I know all about Bonnie and Henrietta."

"Can you believe they got arrested? I might need to have a little sit-down with that husband of yours. Arresting two old ladies like that. And for prostitution, too."

"It wasn't Dylan's call, and they aren't actually arrested. It was Matthew, and he's just bringing them in to scare them into making up is all."

"Oh my. I feel sorry for those deputies, then. I've been around those two when they fight, and it's a sight to see, that's for sure."

She could go on for hours if I let her. "Momma, I'm having a little, I don't know, thing with Dylan."

"A thing? What kind of thing? You mean like an argument?"

"Not exactly an argument, but he did something and it's really bothering me. Has Daddy ever done something that at first you thought was good but then realized he wasn't doing what you thought he was doing?"

"Sweetie, you're going to have to make more sense than that if you want me to help you."

"You heard about Alice Crowder, right?"

"That poor woman. God bless her. She was sweet as could be."

"Dylan thinks her car was stolen by this theft thing, and he asked me to—"

"They took her car too? That's just awful."

"Momma, please."

"Oh yes, go on, sweetie."

"Yes, someone took her car, and Dylan asked me to confirm a story from a woman at the outlet mall. She called for the car to be towed."

"Dylan asked you to work with him? That's a big step for you two, and it's not a step I like. I don't want you putting yourself in any more danger."

"Don't worry. I don't think that was his goal anyway. Turns out the woman's story was already confirmed and it wasn't important to the investigation. I think he did that just to make me feel like I was involved, and I don't know what to do about it."

"What do you mean you don't know what to do about it? It's nice, what he did. He knows how you get and he was probably just trying to include you."

"That's what I thought at first, but he had me do something that didn't matter. Something pointless to the investigation, and I don't know what to do."

"You talk to him, that's what you do."

"I'm too upset with him to talk to him."

"Honey, listen. That man loves you, and he doesn't want anything to happen to you. And let's face it, you do some stupid things, and one of these days that's going to bite you in the behind."

"Gee, thanks."

"Sometimes the truth hurts, honey. I've known that husband of yours since he was knee-high, and if he did what you said, he did it to keep you safe. He didn't do it with ill intent."

"I guess that could be the reason."

"You'll never know unless you talk to him. Just tell him how you feel. Don't let this sit and stir or you'll just tie your stomach up in a ball of knots."

She was right. I did have a tendency to let things fester until I made myself ill.

"Lily? Are you there?"

"I'm here, Momma. You're right. I just need to talk to him about it."

We chatted for a while longer. Mostly she chatted, telling me about my oldest brother's new job, and how Daddy wanted to buy a new pickup truck but she preferred an SUV instead. After thirty minutes, I let her go, using Belle's call as an excuse. Momma could talk the paint off the walls.

"Hey, what's up?"

"I had an interesting conversation with our mortgage guy at the bank today."

I tapped my pencil on the table. "I didn't realize we had a client trying for a loan locally."

"We don't, but they own the paper on the Crowder house and it's in default. He's going into foreclosure if he can't catch up next month."

"Alice said they were having problems, but I didn't know it was that serious."

"There's more. She signed a quitclaim deed last month. She's no longer on the title."

"She signed away her rights to the property? That's an important piece of information. We should let Dylan know."

"I figured you would want to do that."

"I'm not exactly talking to him right now."

"So that's what was bugging you earlier? What happened?"

"It's a long story, and I don't feel like getting into it. Hey, did you hear from Matthew about Bonnie and Henrietta?"

"I did. He said one of the deputies has some video. Thinks it could go viral on YouTube."

"They're not going to—"

She laughed. "No, they're not. Listen, I know you don't want to talk about it, and I don't want to push, but does this thing with Dylan have to do with the Burberry woman?"

"Good guess. The thing is, he's wrong, and I know he's wrong."

"What do you mean?"

"Matthew said they cleared the girl."

"Okay."

"I guess they don't think the car theft thing has anything to do with Alice Crowder's murder, and okay, maybe the Burberry girl didn't have anything to do with it, I don't know, but that doesn't explain who picked it up and how Roger Haines and Mayme Bucklett saw it leaving the day Alice Crowder was killed."

"I'm not sure I understand."

"It's okay, I do. Hey, I gotta go."

"Lily, don't—"

"No, it's fine, really. I'm just not feeling well." I hung up the phone, ran to the bathroom, and lost my entire lunch.

Mary Ripple sat behind the glass in the sheriff's office reception area. She'd been at the job just a few months, but seemed to have a handle on it already. "Hey, Lily, you here to see your hubby or Lucy and Ethel in the holding cell? Those women are a trip, let me tell you."

"Lucy and Ethel?"

"Forget it, it's before your time."

"I was wondering if Bud Crowder was still here?"

"Nope. He's gone. Your husband let him go this morning. I guess the guy he threw the brick at decided not to press charges after all."

"Oh, okay. Thank you."

"You okay, sweetie? You look a little green in the face."

I touched my cheek. "I think I ate something that didn't agree with me."

"You might could have the flu."

"It's probably just something I ate."

"Well, you go on and get some rest."

"Thanks." I would do that, but not before I stopped at Roger Haines's place.

Before I could get to the door, Dylan walked through carrying a paper bag from Millie's.

"Hey. If I'd have known you were coming, I'd have brought you lunch."

I rolled my eyes. "If you think food will help your cause, you're mistaken."

"Oh yeah, about that. I'm—"

"I don't want to talk about it." I walked past him and then turned around. "And you're wrong, by the way."

He started to smile, but furrowed his brow instead.

"What?"

"You look kind of green."

Tears welled up in my eyes. Darn it, I hated crying when I was mad. It made me feel stupid. "I get that way when I'm mad."

"Green?"

"I don't feel well, but don't worry. I'm fine."

"Lily, I'm serious. You don't look good. Maybe you should go home and get some rest." He touched my arm and I yanked it away.

"I said I'm fine."

"Okay. I'll be home soon and we can talk."

"Don't worry. I know you have a murder to solve," I said, and marched out the station's door.

~

Roger Haines and Hughey were playing fetch in his front yard. I pulled into his driveway and Hughey ran over. He'd stopped taking me for a meal and we'd grown to adore each other in a short time.

Roger hollered, "Hughey, heel."

The dog sat in front of my door and brushed his tail back and forth across the driveway. He made me wish Bo had a brother or sister. Don't go there, Lily. My heart was big enough for two dogs, but my house wasn't. I stepped out of the car and squatted next to him. "Hey, Hughey, who's a good boy?"

He swiped his tongue across my cheek, leaving a splatter of sticky slobber.

"I'm sorry about that, but he really seems to like you."

I wiped the excess slobber. "It's fine, really. I've got a boxer mix who drools every time he breathes."

He laughed. "Not surprised to see you here."

"You're not?"

"No, ma'am. You struck me as the kind of woman who sets out to do something and does it."

"I'm going to take that as a compliment. Thank you."

"That's how I meant it. Let me see now, you've come to ask me about my relationship with Alice."

I pressed my lips together, unsure how to respond.

He laughed. "Word gets out quick in this town. But Miss Sprayberry, I loved my wife. Even if she's gone, it doesn't seem right to be with another woman."

My heart believed him, but my head wasn't so sure. Lord knew I'd been fooled by men before, and recently, too. "What would make her husband think you were having an affair?"

"Lots of things, I suppose. Considering the problems they had, maybe I'd feel the same. Men and women can't always be friends, but Alice and I were. She was close with my wife, and like I said, she was there for me after. That bonds people. I guess Bud didn't like it."

"Has he ever said anything about it before?"

He tossed the ball and Hughey ran after it. "A time or two, but not to me. Alice never took it seriously."

"She told you about it?"

"Yes, ma'am. You got to understand, my wife knew things, and she'd tell me them. That's what partners do, they share. I knew Bud wasn't treating her right, knew he hit her a time or two. Knew she was thinking about getting divorced too."

Hughey brought the ball and he tossed it for him again. "Good boy! Go get it!"

"Mr. Haines, do you have any idea who could have done this to Alice?"

He twisted his wedding band around his finger. I hadn't noticed he still had it on. I caught a glimpse of Mayme Bucklett across the street. She'd been tending to her garden when a man I assumed was her husband came out from the garage. They stood and talked, periodically glancing our direction.

"With their financial problems, and Alice's thoughts about divorce, would seem to me Crowder killed her. He went and bought a gun recently too."

I nodded. "That's awful."

"Explains why her car's missing too."

"What do you mean?"

"Bud probably tried to cover his tracks. Stealing the car makes it look like a robbery."

"Are you sure you saw her car that day and not one that looked like hers?"

"Saw her in it every day last week. Waved to her every time she came home from work. Even talked to her through the window, oh, maybe two days before...before she passed."

Nothing made sense. If he saw Alice in her car, then how could the car at the junk yard be hers? Did the person who killed her take the car that day and drive it to the junk yard? Was that who he saw driving the car? And if so, that meant several people were lying about how it got there, and where it was beforehand.

An old pickup truck drove past, and Mr. Haines waved as it pulled up along the side of the road between his house and the Crowder home. "Buddy seems to be handling things better now that his dad is home."

"Seems so. Those rumors about Alice having an affair, do you think there's anything to them?"

"If she was, she never told me about it."

Buddy and another teenage boy went into Buddy's garage and returned carrying two small boxes, which they put in the bed of the truck. I thanked Mr. Haines for talking and rushed over to check on Buddy. "Hey. Just wanted to see how you're doing."

He dipped his head and stared at the ground. "I'm uh…I'm okay."

I smiled at the other boy, who stood on the other side of the truck. "Hi, I'm Lily Sprayberry. And you are?"

"Hank." His facial expression stayed completely blank.

Bingo. "Hi, Hank."

"Hey." He climbed into the truck. "Bud, we got to go."

"Yeah, okay." Buddy tried to smile at me, but failed miserably. "I, uh…I got to go."

"Sure." I pulled a card from my pocket just in case I hadn't given him one before. "Here. If you ever need anything, you just give me a call, okay?"

He eyed the card and then nodded.

"Take care."

The truck pulled down the driveway. I glanced at the house and thought I saw the front window curtain moving, but I wasn't sure. I wasn't about to talk to Bud Crowder, not after I'd just stood outside and talked to the man who had him arrested. Mayme Bucklett was still in her garden, so I headed over there. I wanted to ask her about Alice's car one more time. And if I could, I wanted to talk to her husband, Stew. Maybe he knew something.

"Mrs. Bucklett? Remember me?"

"'Course I remember you. Still see your face all over town."

"I was hoping I could talk to you about the car again."

"Don't got nothing more to say about the car."

Mayme's husband walked out of the garage. He was taller than he looked from across the street, and not a bad-looking guy with his wispy gray hair and freshly shaved face. "Who're you?"

I thrust my hand toward him. "Lily Sprayberry. I was working with Alice Crowder."

"Yeah, the realtor. Wife told me about you."

"I hope she had good things to say."

"Just that you'd been coming around asking questions."

His sour attitude made his attractiveness kind of moot. "Mr. Bucklett, your wife mentioned that you're friendly with Mr. Crowder. I was wondering if you've talked to him since his wife passed?"

"What's all this to you?"

"I was there when their son found her. Had I showed up earlier, I may have been able to, I don't know, stop it, I guess."

His crank expression softened. "I could see how you'd feel like that." He shook his head. "But no, I haven't talked to Crowder. If that happened to me, I'd want to be left alone to deal with it. When he's ready to talk, he'll let me know. He's got enough people buggin' him already, don't you think?"

And the sourness returned. "The town wants to see a murderer caught and brought to justice."

"Then people like you ought to let the police do their job."

I blinked.

"I know about you, Ms. Sprayberry. I know you like to stick your nose into other people's business. I can understand, what with you showing up there like you do, when you did and all, but it might do you some good to keep out of other people's business. Seems like you're doing a disservice to that husband of yours."

My entire body stiffened. "Thanks for your help, Mr. Bucklett. You have a nice day." I took a deep breath and released it before walking back to my car. As I did, I watched Bud Crowder stare at me out the window once again.

CHAPTER 13

I drove around for a while, processing what I'd learned, which wasn't much other than anyone and everyone involved in the case lied about something. I tried to fit the pieces of the puzzle together, but I couldn't. I couldn't fit a square piece into a round hole.

Crime drama shows solved murders in a matter of days, but I didn't think Dylan was close to any arrest. He had Bud Crowder in jail for another crime, but had to let him go. If he'd had anything substantial on the man, he would have kept him for the optional ninety-six hours and tried to get the evidence he needed. But he didn't, and that meant he didn't have a solid case.

Of course, I really didn't know what Dylan was doing, or who he considered suspects because I wasn't exactly talking to him. Not that he would have been honest with me anyway. He'd already proven he'd rather send me on a wild goose chase than take me or anything I did seriously.

I tried to rationalize his position. I tried to see things from his point of view, and sure, I could, to a degree, but not enough to warrant his dishonesty. I felt betrayed. Thinking it through just made me even more frustrated, more angry, more emotional. I cried. I couldn't help it.

I kept driving until I felt a little better. Driving through the pretty countryside, seeing the rolling hills, the pretty colors popping from the warm spring weather, gave me comfort. There wasn't much to Bramblett County, Georgia, not commercially speaking anyway. Though Atlanta's metro area extended all directions, it hadn't quite made it here.

Bramblett was one of the less populated counties on the northern side of the city. We'd recently experienced some growth, families wanting to get out of the urban area in search of a quieter, small-town environment to raise their kids. Our growth hadn't skyrocketed, but it was beginning to pick up speed, and Belle and I had more opportunities for business because of it.

Myrtle Redbecker's property was the first to be purchased and made into a mixed-use development with houses, town-homes, apartments, and retail units. They'd done a great job with the design, and the new property managers added beautiful land-scaping that made the entire area pop. We had two more large plots of land, over two hundred acres each, looking to sell to developers, and Belle signed both as clients a few weeks ago. One already received an offer, and we were just waiting for the county to pre-approve their design plans before closing. Neither Belle nor I were worried it wouldn't happen. It was a sign of things to come. Bramblett County was changing.

Dylan texted me and asked when I'd be home. He said he'd picked up Bo and was waiting for me so we could talk. Murders didn't solve themselves, and I knew he had to get back to work. I told him I'd be home, but first, I had to stop at the drugstore.

～

He met me at the door with a bouquet of flowers and a white balloon with *I love you* printed in sparkly pink. He held them out with a big smile plastered on his face. "Lilies, your favorite."

He knew how to hit me right in the feels. "They're lovely. Thank you." I walked into the kitchen and saw the table set with my momma's fine china. She'd given it to us when we got married.

"Smells good in here, doesn't it?"

My nose was too stuffy to smell anything.

"Here, let me take your stuff."

I held the drugstore bag close to my chest. "It's okay. I've got some medicine in here I need to take." I set it on the small kitchen desk at the far end of the room.

"Good. You've looked sick the past few days."

"You won a few points with the flowers and balloon. Try not to lose them." I smiled so he'd know I was joking, then gave Bo a pat on the head. "Good boy." He hadn't jumped on me at all when I came in. He must have sensed the tension in the house.

"I ordered takeout. I figured apologizing with my own cooking wouldn't do me any favors."

"You barbeque well."

He pulled out my chair and I sat.

"Yes, but that's an all-day affair. Chinese, however, is quick. And I got your favorite."

He opened the white box of sesame chicken, and the smell hit me, making me feel like I was going to be sick again. I sat there for a moment, swallowing and hoping the feeling would pass, but it didn't. I scrambled out of my chair and ran to the bathroom.

Bo sat next to me on the bathroom floor, his body leaning into mine. He did that when he was scared. Poor guy.

Dylan helped me up. "Bad idea to get Chinese?"

"The smell, I guess it just hit me wrong."

"It's okay. I'll take it back to work so you don't have to keep smelling it. Let's get you into your pajamas and into bed."

He guided me toward the bed, and I yanked a tissue from the box on my nightstand. I wiped the tears on my cheeks and the sides of my mouth while he pulled off my boots.

"The flu's going around. The amount of people you're around every day, I wouldn't be surprised if you've got it."

He helped me into my pajamas and got me tucked into bed. I didn't complain. He was right, I felt awful. Bo lay beside me, pressing his big warm body into mine. It made me sweat, but it was comforting too.

"Bo, come on, I need a little space." I pushed at him, but he did a fabulous imitation of a boulder and wouldn't budge.

Dylan raised his brow and then rounded the other side of the bed to tug him away from me. Bo didn't argue, but he didn't make it easy for Dylan to move him either.

My husband sat on my side of the bed and felt my forehead. "You don't have a fever. Want me to go ahead and leave the food here?"

Just hearing the word food made me want to heave again. "Please don't say that word again."

He laughed. "I'll get you a glass of water. You're probably not up for talking, but I did want to tell you I'm sorry. I wasn't trying to hurt you, Lily. I was trying to protect you. I hope you know that."

The thing was, deep down, I did know that. But the less deep down part of me was still upset about it. "I know."

"So you forgive me."

I tucked my arm under my pillow. "Not yet, but I will. Eventually." I was just too tired and ill to care. I caught him smiling as I closed my eyes.

"I won't be home until late, but text or call if you need something, okay?"

"Okay."

"We're making an arrest tonight."

I sat up. "For Alice's murder? Who?"

"Her husband did it, Lily. We matched the bullets from his gun to the one we found at the scene. The one that went through her hand."

"Oh, wow. I guess he really did think she was having an affair."

"We learned they had some serious financial problems, and just a month ago he'd taken a million-dollar life insurance policy out on his wife. Probably thought that would solve all his money problems."

"He also got her to sign a quitclaim deed recently, and their house is almost in foreclosure."

"I didn't know about the quitclaim deed."

I lay back down, and my head sank into my pillow. "There's more to the car thing, though. I know you don't think so, but there is."

"We'll talk about that when you're feeling better, okay?" He kissed me on the forehead, and within seconds, I was out.

$\sim$

Belle darted out of Millie's and smacked the hood of my car just as I put it in park. "You are not going to believe this!"

"Did you just put a dent in my hood?"

She whipped around and examined it. "No." Then she practically yanked me into the café. Now hurry, this is big."

I smoothed down the wrinkles taking over the top half of my pink and white striped button down shirt. The inside of the café smelled of overripe strawberries. "What's going on?"

Old Man Goodson and Billy Ray Brownlee wobbled up from their seats at my usual back table.

"We've come to a decision," Billy Ray said.

Belle golf-clapped. "And it's a good one!"

Millie topped off the men's coffee. "It better work, that's all I got to say. I understand Bonnie's problems with Henrietta. Last night I found a pair of her underwear on the kitchen table. And it wasn't freshly washed."

Belle shivered. "Ew."

"You're telling me." Millie smiled and lightly touched my arm. "Coffee and a scone this morning, Lily Bit? I made strawberry ones."

I could smell them. "Oh, no thank you. I'd love a chamomile tea, though, if it's not too much trouble."

She backed away. "You sick still? Don't breathe on me, then. I can't afford to be sick. I'm an employee down at the moment."

I covered my mouth. "I'm fine. Just not ready to shock my stomach quite yet." I sat at the table and set my bag beside my legs. "So, what's this decision you've made?"

Billy Ray puffed out his chest. "We're moving to Alabama."

I blinked. "Excuse me?"

"Yuppers, me and Old Man Goodson here are up and moving to find us some new lady friends."

Belle leaned toward me. "They hear the women there aren't as, shall we say, malicious as they are here."

My head shifted between the men and Belle. "Are you serious?"

Old Man Goodson placed his hand on my knee. "Now, darling, you think I'd up and leave you like that? We've been through a lot, you and me, and you're kin to me now, like a daughter."

"I'm confused. Are you moving or not?"

"We're pretending to move. Telling the women we're tired of their little fight, and we're heading to Alabama to find us some new friends," he said.

My mouth opened into a circle and then spread to a huge smile. "Really? I love that."

Belle threw her hands above her head. "Right? They're going to lose their minds. I can't wait."

Billy Ray leaned into Old Man Goodson's arm and whispered, "I think Belle here is liking this a little too much."

"I'm just tired of all this. If anything's going to get those women reunited, it's going to be the panic of losing you two."

"She's right about that," Millie said, setting my tea in front of me. "Here you go, sweetie."

"Thank you."

"Okay, I need to know, who thought this up?"

Billy Ray tapped his index finger into his chest. "Sort of. One of the boys at the fire department, he told me he had himself a date with some hottie he met on that internet dating site all you young people use."

"I have never used an internet dating site," I said.

Belle raised her hand. "Ditto."

"He said I might could make myself a page and get me a lady friend too. Told him I had two, but they'd been fighting something fierce lately, and I was tired of it. He said he knew about that, said the whole county knows about it. So, he showed me a dating site for people my age. Something called Silver Singles, and it gave me the idea."

Belle chuckled. "It's a fifty-and-over site."

"And we're over fifty," he said.

"That you are," Millie said. She laughed and walked away to help a customer.

"So, how are you going to make this work?" I asked.

Billy Ray shrugged. "Don't ask me." He hitched his thumb toward Old Man Goodson. "He's the details guy."

"The plan is to tell the ladies we're leaving to go find us a place to live, and once we get one, we'll come back and move our stuff. Really, we're going fishing on Lake Lanier, but they don't need to know that."

I smiled again. "I love that. I think it'll work. Belle's right. If there's anything that'll reunite those two, it's the two of you. No way will they want to share you with anyone."

Billy Ray nodded. "That's for sure. Before all this willy wolly happened, the lady who works the register at the Walmart smiled at me, and Bonnie about climbed over the counter to get at her." A slow smile crept across his face, highlighting the spot where his bottom front tooth once was. "I had to pull her off. Last thing I need is getting banned from the Walmart. I get my Old Spice there."

"Oh, I know that stuff," Belle said.

"Your daddy wear it?" Old Man Goodson asked.

"No, my grandpa." She noticed the expressions on the men's faces. "I love the smell."

Bonnie tapped on the café window, and Belle pointed to her. We all flipped toward the window. She held up her hand and brought it to her mouth, then put it down again. She did that several times. I knew she wanted a cup of coffee, but I kind of got a kick out of her cute little version of charades.

"I think she wants something to drink," Billy Ray said.

"Looks like it," Old Man Goodson replied. He sipped his own cup of coffee.

"We might could get her a cup."

"Maybe in a few minutes. Let's let her suffer a bit."

I leaned my head onto Old Man Goodson's shoulder. "That's pretty harsh."

"Got to play hard ball when you're making a point."

As Bonnie became increasingly frustrated, her hand motions intensified. We all adjusted our positions to ignore her.

"Oh for the love of Jesus, y'all are awful." Millie marched over to the door and opened it. "Get on in here. Just behave yourself, or I'll throw you out on your butt like the sheriff did."

Bonnie walked in, her chin up and pointing away from us. She didn't even look our direction.

Old Man Goodson stretched, groaning loudly. "I guess it's time." He glanced at Billy Ray. "You coming?"

"Where?"

"To tell Bonnie our news. That's where."

"Oh yeah. I plumb forgot already." He took a few extra seconds to maneuver out of the chair. A stalling technique, I figured.

Bonnie sat at the table opposite us, facing away.

"Oh boy." Belle pointed to the café entrance. "Anyone got Iron Man's cell?"

Old Man Goodson and Billy Ray froze, staring at the window in what looked like sheer fear.

Billy Ray laughed. "Ain't no Iron Man going to save that woman."

"I'm not trying to save them. I'm trying to save us."

CHAPTER 14

*M*illie marched over from behind the counter and let Henrietta in. She stomped back to the counter, flipped around, and informed the entire small café of her feelings. "Now you listen here, all of you. This is my café, and I make the rules. I let you two battling biddies in because your men over here got something to tell you, but if either of you pitch a fit or start a fight, I'll throw you out with my own bare hands, you hear?" She pointed her finger at the rest of the customers. "And all y'all, if you encourage them, I'll throw you out too."

"Something to tell us?" Henrietta said. "What's she talking about? You two finally decide whose side you're on?"

Old Man Goodson took Henrietta's arm and led her to the same table as Bonnie.

"You ain't gonna put her at my table, are you?"

"Yes, Bonnie, I am. Now you hush. We got some important news."

The two women looked at each other, and I could have sworn I saw an emotional connection. It was brief, and tiny, but it was there. Progress.

"Me and Billy Ray, we've had enough. We can't beg or plead,

or force you two ladies to do anything. Lord knows we've tried, but the good man above, he can't make that kind of miracle happen, reuniting you two. And we know it, so we made a decision. Billy Ray here's got a friend who signed us up for one of them singles sites on the world wide web, and we've got us some new gals, and we're moving to Alabama. Matter of fact, we're heading out there today to find us a place to live."

The two women's mouths dropped.

"What in God's creation are you talking about?" Henrietta asked.

Bonnie nodded. "Yeah, what she said."

"I said, we're moving to Alabama."

Billy Ray chimed in, his voice shaky and cracking. "For the ladies."

Bonnie and Henrietta stared at each other, both silent but very likely brewing a hissy fit internally.

"This is your fault," Bonnie finally said.

"My fault? You're the one who kicked me out. It's your fault."

"All you got to do is apologize, and you can't even do that."

"What? I did apologize. I even said nice things about you, but I take all that back."

Bonnie crossed her arms. "I don't remember no apology. I remember you said you didn't need to apologize."

I kind of remembered it that way too, but I kept my mouth shut. I didn't want to get in the middle of that!

"See, this is why we're leaving. We met us some women on the world wide web—"

Belle coughed. "Internet."

Old Man Goodson turned and looked at her, then turned back to the ladies. "Internet. We met some ladies through the internet, and we're moving to Alabama to get to know them. We're done worrying about, as Millie says, you battling biddies."

Their eyes widened.

"Did you hear what he called us?" Bonnie asked.

Henrietta nodded. "I did."

"You may be a biddy, but not me. I'm a former southern belle."

Belle swallowed so hard I heard the gulp. "Oh boy."

"Hey." I stood and planted myself in front of the men. "Remember what Millie said? I'm sure we can all discuss this without throwing insults at one another."

Bonnie interrupted me before I could start my next sentence. "My men are threatening to leave. I got to defend my rights here."

Henrietta threw her hands up in the air, her face reddening. "Your men? They're mine! You just get my sloppy seconds."

Belle coughed again.

Millie had given them both cups of coffee, but snatched them off the table, spilling most of Bonnie's in the process. "All right. All right. I gave y'all a chance, but you couldn't do it, could you? You couldn't act like adults." She held her arm out toward the rest of the café. "You're upsetting my customers. Look at them shaking in their seats."

Ronnie Chastain, the local pharmacist, held up his hand. "Uh, I'm not shaking."

"Neither am I," his pharmacy tech said. "I'm kind of enjoying this."

Melba Bailey, a café regular, raised her hand. "It's better than my daytime soap opera. More real-life like."

I bit my lip.

"I don't care. I don't like it, and I don't have to have it in my café. Now out. And don't you come back until you two can at least be civil to each other, and I mean it."

Henrietta was the first to up and leave, marching out—as much as a woman who sometimes used a cane could march—as tears fell from her eyes. Bonnie followed, rubbing her eyes and muttering something about pigs flying. She let the door slam behind her.

Billy Ray took a swig of his now lukewarm coffee. "I think that worked. How 'bout you, Old Man?"

A grin spread across Old Man Goodson's face. I was pretty sure I saw a little glint of sparkle in his eyes, too. "I'd say so."

Leaning back in her chair and laughing, Belle sipped her drink and said, "I'm not so sure about that, but it's not my call."

Old Man Goodson added another packet of sugar to his drink. "You just wait now. You'll see."

A while back, I'd learned Old Man Goodson always had something up his sleeve, so I didn't question his actions.

Belle and I spent the morning in the office reviewing client options, setting appointments, and critiquing our recent advertising promotions. I loved them, of course, like I did every piece of advertising Belle put together. But she wasn't pleased with her latest work, and we decided to scratch it and start over. Really, she decided, and I just went along with her.

"I just don't like the font. And the colors. And I think the approach is wrong. Plus, our photo is cheesy, don't you think? I hate these traditional real estate professional photographs. We need something different, something unique that sets us apart from everyone else."

I stared at the mock brochure she'd created, but I wasn't paying attention to Belle. I heard her voice, but the words didn't quite sink in. The car, that's what I kept coming back to. The car. It was key to the whole murder, and something told me Hank Dean was involved with it. I had no evidence to prove he was, but I didn't have any to prove he wasn't, either.

"And then I took off all my clothes and ran around the store screaming, *It's the UFO! It's coming for us all!*"

I blinked. "I'm sorry, what?"

Belle huffed. "You didn't hear a thing I said, did you?"

"I'm sorry. My mind wandered."

She tapped her pencil on our conference table. "Right, your mind wandered. Is it Dylan or what?"

"It's nothing. I'm just tired, and my stomach's been bothering me lately. You know that. But I'm feeling much better today. I didn't wake up nauseous this morning for a change."

The pencil dropped from her hand, hit the table, and rolled off the edge. "No." She pushed her chair back from the table. "Oh my God, Lily! You're pregnant!"

"What? No. No, I had a bug, but it's gone." I slid a file toward her side of the table. "Now come on, sit down. We have work to do."

"Are you late? This is why you've been such a hot mess lately. I knew something was up. Does Dylan know? Have you taken a test?"

"Settle down there, partner. I'm not late."

She pressed her lips together and raised her eyebrows as she sat back down. She bent over and picked up the pencil, tapping it vigorously on the table.

"Belle."

"What?"

"The pencil."

She tapped harder. "What? Does it bother you? Are you getting annoyed? That's a sign too, you know. Are you craving pickles? Ice cream maybe?"

"I hate pickles and you know it."

"Caroline hated pickles too, and when she was pregnant she ate like a thousand of them, remember?"

"I remember, and I'm not pregnant, so don't go rushing off to get me jars of pickles."

She stopped tapping the pencil, instead pounding the ball of her foot on our thin carpet. Pound. Pound. Pound.

I exhaled. "Can you make the changes to the Cuttahey listing?

I'll go pick up the signage from the Bryants' place. I've got to go out that way anyway."

"I'm getting you a pregnancy test. I can come over tonight and be with you while you take it."

"You going to watch me pee on a stick? The woman who gags at the thought of public restrooms because of the smell?"

"Ew. Did you have to mention that?"

I smiled, hoping the change in attitude would convince her. "I promise you, *when* Dylan and I decide to have a baby, you'll be the first to know, and I swear that time is not now. We haven't even talked about it."

"Accidents happen. I was one, remember?"

"You were not."

"I was. I mean, obviously my parents were already married and all, but they hadn't expected to have another kid and then—" She raised her arm in the air and waved. "Surprise! I showed up!"

"Yeah, but you know me. I hate surprises."

"Tell that to the baby in your belly." She rubbed her hands together. "I'm so excited."

"Belle, stop. I had a bug, that's all."

"Fine. Whatever you say, Miss Queen of Denial."

"Whatever." I shuffled the papers in front of me into a pile. "Now I'm off to pick up some signs. See you in a few hours?"

"Yes, ma'am."

I stopped for a to-go coffee from Millie's, mostly to check on her and make sure she was okay, which she was. I wanted to be able to drink it, but was pretty sure I couldn't. I'd just lost the taste for the stuff.

She straightened the plastic-wrapped brownies on the counter. "I'm over their little tiff. They want to act like brats, then let them. They're just not doing it in my café."

"Hopefully the men's idea works. They did seem pretty upset at the news."

"They did. It was the most fun I've had in months, watching

them get their undies all twisted in a knot like that." She handed me my coffee. "Between us, that Henrietta's beginning to cramp my style."

I swallowed hard. "Oh, well...I..."

She winked at me. "Cat got your tongue there, Lily?"

I held up my thumb and index finger in an inch sign. "Maybe a little."

I hesitantly sipped the coffee, hoping my stomach reacted appropriately. But it didn't get much of a chance. My taste buds just weren't interested. I set it on the counter. "I think I need a tea instead."

She tilted her head. "Coming right up."

As she prepared my tea, my cell phone beeped with a message from Buddy Crowder, asking me to meet him. When I asked why he wasn't in school, he responded that he was but would leave. I invited him to Millie's but he asked for someplace more private, so I suggested the dog park. There were enough benches for us to sit and chat without others paying attention.

He said he'd be there in fifteen minutes, so I chatted with Millie a bit longer, then headed over to the park.

As Buddy walked toward me, he kept his head low and his hood pulled up. It wasn't warm outside, but it wasn't cold enough to require a thick coat and hood. Buddy Crowder didn't want to be seen with me.

Or at least that's what I thought.

He sat next to me. "Hey."

"Hey. You okay?"

"I think I know who killed my mom."

CHAPTER 15

"Should I get the sheriff here?"

"I don't know what to do. He arrested my dad, but he didn't kill her, Miss Lily, I know he didn't." His jaw was clenched, and I could see the tendons in his neck bulging.

"Buddy." I shifted on the bench to face him. "Tell me what's going on, and I'll try to help."

He rocked in place. "My mom's car. You know how it wasn't there?"

I nodded, but kept my mouth shut and let him speak. That's what they did on crime dramas, and even if they were fake, it worked in home sales, so I had a feeling it would work with him too.

"It…it wasn't stolen. I know y'all think it was, but it was a setup, and my mom, she found out, and I think that's why they killed her."

I exhaled. "Go on."

He jumped from the bench and paced back and forth in front of me. "My dad didn't do it, okay? He didn't kill my mom."

I stood and tried to calm him. "Let's not let the whole county hear you, okay? Come on, sit and start from the beginning."

He took a deep breath. "So, I heard my mom talking to our neighbor, and I heard her say money was tight, and she didn't know if they could afford the house payment."

"Okay."

"Yeah, then she said she didn't want to lose it, so she was gonna call you so she could sell it."

"Okay."

"And my friend Hank, you know. His dad works at an auto shop."

"The sheriff talked to Hank and his father, Buddy. He cleared them of any involvement."

"But he's wrong. They are involved, and it's my fault."

I was more confused than before. "I don't understand."

He wrapped his arms around his body and rocked. "I...I told Hank we were having problems, and he brought me to his dad. They said they could get cash fast, and told me how."

"How?"

"We'd get the car and bring it to Hank's dad's junk yard. They got these shops to go along with it for a cut of the cash. And then this girl at the mall, she'd call and say the car was abandoned in the lot, so a tow guy would get it, and they'd say they sat on it for a few days, then brought it to the junk yard."

"Okay, so did any of that happen?"

"Sort of. I don't know, it's all so confusing."

"It's okay. Take your time."

"Hank's dad said the guy they worked for, he wanted a paper trail in case something happened. They wanted it clean. I don't know what that means."

"Okay, let me get this straight. You brought the car to the junk yard, but said you brought it to a shop?"

He nodded.

"So, the shop never got the car, but they have paperwork that says they did, and that someone picked it up. Then the girl at the outlet mall calls a towing company, says there's an abandoned car in the lot, and they come and tow it. But that didn't really happen because the car wasn't even at the mall?"

"Yeah."

"And how was this supposed to get you money?"

"Hank's dad said they strip the car and sell it for parts. He said the guy who sells the parts splits the cash with everyone, and he'd get me in on the deal too so I could help my mom."

Oh boy. "Is that what you did?"

"Yeah."

"Okay, explain to me how you got the car to the shop in the first place."

"Hank brought over a bad battery and we switched it out. When my mom tried to go to work the next morning, it wouldn't start, so I called Hank, and he gave her a jump. I offered to take her to work and then drop the car off at the shop. Said I'd have Hank follow and bring me to school."

"But your neighbors saw the car the day your mom was killed."

He nodded. "I know. It was someone from the junk yard. They killed my mom. I know it."

"I don't understand."

"That day, my mom was driving her route, and she saw her car. She called me about it. Said she was going to ask Mr. Haines to bring her to the shop because she was mad they were driving it around. She said they shouldn't have had it that long anyway, and they weren't telling her what was wrong with it, just that they didn't think it was the battery.

"I told her they had to test it, but she wouldn't listen. She was going to get it. I asked Hank to take me home right away, but he kept screwing around, taking his time. He heard me talking to my mom about it, and I think he told his dad. When we were driving to my house, I saw the car driving down the street."

"Did you see who was driving?"

He shook his head. "They had on a baseball cap."

"Did Hank go into the house with you?"

"Yeah, but he didn't stay. He just dropped me off and took off. Said he had stuff to do. He didn't even go downstairs. I lied about that. I don't know why. But now I think he…I think he knew something was up."

"You think your mom called the shop and somehow found out what? That it wasn't there?"

"I don't know, but whatever she did, I think they were gonna get busted, so they killed her."

"Do you have any idea who might have come to your house? Any idea at all?"

He dropped his head and nodded slowly.

"You have to tell me, Buddy. You know that."

"I think it was Hank's dad."

I exhaled a breath I didn't even know I'd been holding. "Okay. Does Hank know you skipped classes today?"

"I mean, yeah. He'll see I'm not there."

"Okay. Here's what we're going to do."

I laid out a quick plan, and we hurried to my car.

Mary Ripple smiled brightly when we walked into the sheriff's office. "Well isn't this a pleasure? Twice in one week. And you're looking better too."

I smiled. "Thanks, I feel better. Is my husband in?"

Buddy stared at me.

"He sure is, honey. Let me call him."

She pressed a button on her phone. "Sheriff Roberts, you have a lovely young lady waiting for you at the front desk."

Buddy whispered, "You're married to the sheriff?"

I smiled but didn't look at him. "I have connections."

Dylan's smile faded when he saw Buddy Crowder. "His dad's being processed. He can't see him yet."

"We're not here for his dad."

He furrowed his brow. "Okay, come on back."

Buddy repeated his story to Dylan, adding a few extra details he'd left out earlier.

Dylan ran his hand over the top of his short hair and glanced at me. "And you just found all of this out?"

I nodded.

He pressed a button on his phone and asked Mary to send in Deputy Riley.

Matthew walked in, looking surprised to see me with Buddy Crowder. "We, uh, Crowder's not ready for visitors yet."

"We're going to need to put that on hold."

"On hold?"

Dylan nodded. "Keep him in a holding cell for now. I need bodies at the outlet mall and..." He flipped through his note pad and named off the two auto shops. "And the junk yard too." He gave Matthew specific instructions, and he rushed out.

Buddy twisted his fingers together. "Can I, uh...can I see my dad?"

Dylan used a calm, soft voice, much different from the authoritative one he'd just used with Matthew. "Give them a few minutes to get him situated and we'll see, okay?"

"Yes, sir."

I made eye contact with Dylan and flicked my head toward the door. "Can you take me to the ladies' room, please?"

He nodded. "Buddy, you want something to drink? We've got Coke, stale coffee, water."

"A Coke would be cool, yeah."

We stepped out of his office and he closed the door.

"What's going to happen to Buddy?"

He rubbed the back of his neck. "If what he says pans out, we're going to have to charge him."

I grimaced. "But he told you what happened. Can't you give him a break?"

"I can try, but it's not up to me. It's up to the district attorney."

"What about his dad? Are you going to release him?"

"The bullets matched his, Lily."

"The killer could have used his gun. Did he have the gun on him when he left?"

"He swears he didn't."

"Then where was it?"

"In his nightstand drawer."

"So he still could have come home and used it. I get it, but a nightstand is a logical place for a gun. Everyone knows that. Someone else could have looked there and found it. You can't rule that out."

He grabbed a Coke from the employee lounge. "If they'd gone there with the intent to kill her, they would have brought their own weapon, and even if they didn't, I'm not sure they'd have the sense to wipe it clean and put it back where they found it." He exhaled. "It still looks bad for the husband, honey."

"But what about everything Buddy said?"

"We still can't account for Crowder at the time of his wife's death, and his neighbor thinks he saw his vehicle on the street that day."

"Which neighbor? That Bucklett woman?"

"Roger Haines."

Haines never mentioned that to me. "Then who was driving her car after she was killed? Two neighbors said they saw it, and now you've got Buddy saying he did too. Isn't that worth something?"

"We have the gun, and we have motive."

"You have two motives. A car theft ring was about to be called out. That's big stuff, right? Something someone would kill over to keep hidden?"

"It's possible. We're going to talk to the husband. You heard me. I've got guys going out to the auto shops. They'll bring them in, and we'll interrogate them too. We'll figure it out, Lily." He opened his office door.

The fear in Buddy's eyes got to me. "Hey, how you doing?"

"Okay, I guess."

Dylan walked in and closed the door. "I'm going to need you to stay put while we bring in the others, okay?"

"Can, uh…can she stay with me?"

I grabbed a hold of his hand and squeezed. "Of course, I can."

Dylan's eyes narrowed just enough for me to notice. "Yeah, she can stay. I'll set you two up in a conference room. You got a phone, son?"

"Yes, sir."

"I'd like to keep that for now, okay?"

Buddy looked at me for approval. "It's okay," I said.

He handed Dylan his phone, and Dylan got us set up in a conference room. I texted Belle and let her know what was going on and that I'd keep her posted.

Buddy sat at the table with his head down for several minutes before finally asking, "I'm in trouble, aren't I?"

I closed my eyes, breathed in, and then blew out the breath as I opened them. "I'm not sure what's going to happen."

"But you're the sheriff's wife."

"That doesn't mean I know the fine details of the laws."

"But you think I'm in trouble."

I didn't want to lie to him, but I didn't want him any more upset than he was already. "I think it's best to wait and see what happens."

He sank lower into the chair. "I was just trying to help. We got insurance on the car. They would have got my mom a new one."

I'd been pacing the room, but I stopped. "You know what? Let me ask my husband something." I walked to the other side of the table and tried to twist the door handle, but it was locked. "Great." I pressed the button on the phone sitting on the table.

Mary's voice came through the speaker. "Yes, Mrs. Roberts?"

Did nobody in the town notice I hadn't changed my name? "Can you send my husband, please?"

"All righty. Just a moment."

Five minutes later, and I knew it was five because I watched the numbers on my iWatch tick by, he showed up.

I pursed my lips when he smiled at me, and the smile disappeared. "You locked us in."

"Sorry. It's a habit." The corner of his mouth twitched, but at that moment I didn't find it all that appealing.

I pointed to the door. "Can we…"

He held it open. "Lead the way, Mrs. Roberts."

I dragged him to his office and slammed the door behind us. "I'm fixin to throw a hissy fit right now."

"That's apparent."

CHAPTER 16

*T*he darn mouth twitch thing happened again.

"Stop that."

He smirked. "Stop what?"

I pointed at his mouth. "That…that twitchy thing you do when you think you're being cute."

"I always think I'm being cute." Twitch. Twitch.

I squeezed my fists into tight balls, digging my too-long nails into my palms. My temper skyrocketed. "First, I don't appreciate being held prisoner by my husband, and second…" I flung my hand at the door. "Can't you tell these people I didn't change my name or something?"

Slight smile and another twitch.

I groaned. "This isn't funny."

"But it kind of is."

I leaned my backside against his desk and crossed my arms over my chest. "You're wrong."

"First." He walked closer to me. "I locked the door out of habit. I apologize for that. And second." He stepped closer until he was almost touching me. He lifted my chin and forced me to look at him.

My mouth wanted to smile, and I had to fight it.

"I kind of like it when people call you Mrs. Roberts."

Well, darn. My mouth betrayed me with a smile.

He kissed me gently. "But I'll remind them if you'd like."

"I hate it when you do that."

"Do what?"

"Be all cute and stuff when I'm mad at you."

"I've been practicing since I was eight."

I rolled my eyes.

"Was there a reason you needed to see me, or did you just want to yell at me?"

"A little of both."

He chuckled.

"Does Crowder have an attorney?"

"He does."

"Can you bring him in to talk to Buddy?"

"Did he ask for him?"

"No, but I don't think he knows to."

"We can't bring him an attorney unless he or the attorney asks."

"Okay, then I'll make sure he asks." I adjusted the collar of his shirt. "Does his dad know what's going on?"

"Not yet. Hey, it's lunch time. Why don't I order you something from Millie's? I'll get the kid something too. We'll get the suspects in, and I'll get my guys on them."

"Fine, I'll see what he wants, but can you keep the door unlocked, please?"

"Yes, ma'am."

We walked over to Mary, and Dylan made arrangements for her to get us lunch. "Lily will come back with their order."

"Oh honey, just call me on speaker, and I'll write it down. No need to bother making another trip up here."

"Thank you."

I got our orders and called her on the intercom.

"I'll have someone get it right quick, honey."

"Thank you. Oh, and can you add a pickle to my order?"

"Sure thing, sweetie."

Fifteen minutes later, Buddy Crowder asked to see his dad's attorney.

Buddy was released under his aunt's supervision. I assured him I'd keep in touch and was available if he needed something. His aunt lived about an hour away in Fulton County, and I hoped no one could touch him there, though Dylan promised me no one told any of the men they arrested how they found out.

As I left the department, I saw the woman from the outlet mall sitting at Matthew's desk, her arm cuffed to the chair. When she saw me, her look of surprise quickly changed to agitation.

I smiled at her. "Oh, I just remembered, I need to return those gloves."

~

Belle met me at Millie's again, and the three of us traded theories on the fight between Henrietta and Bonnie before I filled them in on what was happening with the Crowder case.

Millie took a bite of scone and talked with her mouth full. "You ask me, the kid did it."

"Which kid?" I asked.

"The son. You know it's always a family member."

"It's not always a family member, and besides, I've talked to him. I don't think he did it. He was genuinely upset about everything."

I picked off a piece of her scone and popped it into my mouth. "Oh, this is good. Blueberry?"

"Yes, ma'am."

Having an appetite again felt wonderful.

"You can kill someone and be upset about it. Especially if that someone's your momma," Millie said.

"It's not just that. He came to me out of fear, not so much out of regret. I don't know how to explain it, it's just a gut feeling."

"Aw." Belle wrapped her arm around my shoulder. "You're going to make a great momma."

I broke away from her and shot her a steely stare. "Someday, but not anytime soon."

"I checked with Henrietta, and she's flipping her lid about the men." Millie giggled.

"I got a voicemail from Bonnie about an hour ago," Belle said, sipping her coffee like she had the rest of the day to drink it. "I haven't called her back yet. Figured I'd let her sweat it out."

I smiled. "What'd she say?"

She pulled her phone from her pocket and played us the message on speaker.

"Belle, it's Bonnie. Are you there? Hello? Am I supposed to talk after that beep? I don't know if you can hear this or not, but we got to stop those boys from meeting them floozies in Alabama. Don't they know what those women are like out there? They cook squirrel stew for cryin' out loud. Billy Ray's stomach can't handle no squirrel stew. Call me back. It's Bonnie in case you forgot. Bye now."

"My momma used to make squirrel stew," Millie said.

My lunch rushed up my throat. I slid the chair back, covered my mouth, and muttered, "Excuse me," as I ran to the bathroom.

I heard Millie say, "I told her not to get me sick," as I ran.

So much for feeling better.

I wiped my mouth clean and dabbed a paper towel at the corners of my eyes, then sipped a little water from the faucet. My mouth tasted like pickle. What in the blazes made me even want a pickle? I totally regretted that. Pickles did not taste all that good going down, and they tasted a heck of a lot worse coming back up.

When I walked back from the bathroom, Belle eyed me suspiciously. "You okay?"

I sat back down and nodded. "I'm *fine*. I tried an experiment today and it failed."

Millie was at the counter taking an order.

Belle raised an eyebrow. "What kind of experiment?"

"I tried a pickle, and I hated it."

She tried hard not to smile, but failed.

"That proves your theory is wrong." I leaned closer to her and whispered, "You know all pregnant women love pickles."

"If that's what you have to tell yourself, then fine."

"Anyway." I changed the subject back to what mattered. "You should call Bonnie back."

She shook her head. "The men want us to wait until tomorrow morning. They're pretty sure Bonnie and Henrietta will have lost their minds by then."

"They're pretty confident in themselves if they think it's going to happen that fast."

She shrugged. "I didn't ask why they thought it. I didn't want those details."

I sipped my drink. "You and me both."

My phone chimed with Dylan's text notification. I read it and smiled. "He's letting Bud Crowder go."

"He is?"

I nodded. "The DA doesn't think they've got a strong enough case yet. I guess the stuff Buddy told him panned out or something." I tapped a quick response and waited. When he replied, I relayed the information to Belle. "He says the auto theft is a game changer, and they're working that angle." I smiled. "I guess someone could look in a nightstand after all."

"What?"

I laughed. "Nothing. Just my amazing investigation skills at work again."

She nodded. "All right then."

CHAPTER 17

I woke up on the couch to Bo barking his head off and a pounding on my side door. It took me a second to figure out what the pounding was, and when I heard Bonnie hollering between each of them, I bounded off the couch and bolted to the door. I checked the clock. Eleven-fifteen.

"Bo, sit."

He sat next to the kitchen table.

I yanked the door open. "Are you okay?"

Henrietta, standing behind Bonnie, popped her head around her. "We need help saving our men."

I smiled. "It's after eleven. Can't this wait until the morning?"

"A girl's got to do what a girl's got to do," Bonnie said.

"You mean two girls." Henrietta moved beside Bonnie and grabbed her hand.

If I weren't so tired, I would have jumped for joy. Who'd have thought the men's plan would work, and that quickly too.

Bo barked. I turned around and smiled at him. "Oh, sorry, buddy." I released him from sitting with a quick "okay," then held the door open for the women. "I'm awake now, so you might as well come on in."

I closed the door behind them.

"Is your hubby sleeping?"

"He's still at work. They've had a break in the Crowder case."

Henrietta tilted her head. "Crowder case? What happened? Did I hear about it?"

"I'm sure you have. You've just been a little distracted lately."

Bonnie took a coffee pod from the holder and stared at the Keurig. "Where's the pot?"

I took the pod and stuffed it into the holder, filled the canister, and started the machine as I got a cup from the cabinet. "There's no pot. It only makes one cup at a time."

"What's the point of that? I shouldn't have to make a cup of coffee every time I want one when I can just pour a cup from a big pot full of the stuff."

"Because some people like a consistent flavor to their coffee."

"Mine's consistent. I poop every time I drink it."

Henrietta giggled. "She ain't lyin'."

I rolled my eyes. "Okay, why me? Why not Belle?" I eyed Henrietta. "Or Millie? You live with her already."

"Not no more. I'm back with my bestie now. Besides, you're the smart one of the group."

Score one for the boys. That was definitely a big win for them, the two living together again.

"Okay, then what do you need from me?" I finished making Bonnie's coffee. "You want one?" I asked Henrietta.

"No, I'm good. I just want our men back."

I sat between them at the table, rubbing Bo's ears. "And exactly how do you plan to do that?"

Bonnie's eyes widened, and she smiled. "We thought your hubby could get us one of those things that follows people. Maybe stick it on their car or something. You know, so we can find them."

"A tracking device? That would have worked if you'd thought

of it before they left, but they're long gone now. They were going to look for a place, remember?"

Bonnie's shoulders sank. "Well dang."

"What about one of them phone trackers? I saw something on *Law & Order* where they did something to the towers where the calls come from, and they got their robber." She pressed her lips together and closed one eye. "I'm not sure how they did it, though, but I figure Dylan's got to know."

Dylan's car pulled into the driveway. "Speak of the devil." I flicked my chin toward the small window next to the door. "Why don't you ask him about it yourself?"

Dylan walked in cautiously, and Bo jumped up on him like he hadn't seen him in weeks. "Hey, buddy." He patted his head. "Off, please." He smiled at the ladies. "Kind of late for happy hour, isn't it?"

"They want their men back."

"Yeah, we need to save them from those Alabama floozies," Henrietta said.

"Billy Ray's got him a sensitive stomach. He can't eat that food they cook out there."

Dylan tried not to smile. "You mean barbecue?"

"Barbecued squirrel is more like it."

I swallowed hard and held up my hand. "Please, don't be specific."

Bonnie nodded. "See? No one can stomach that stuff."

Dylan grabbed a beer from the fridge and looked at me. "Did I know they went to Alabama?"

I shook my head. "I forgot to mention it."

He smiled. "Ladies, nothing personal, but with the way you've been acting, I might have packed up and beat it too. But don't worry, I'm sure they'll be back soon."

"They won't be," Bonnie cried. "That's the thing. They met some floozies on the internet. My grandson says it's probably some sex chat box or something."

The corner of Dylan's mouth twitched, and this time, my heart fluttered.

"Room," I said. "Chat room, and I'm sure that's not at all what happened."

"Well, something like that happened because they're moving there to replace us."

Dylan undid the top button of his shirt and disconnected the radio from his shoulder. "Maybe you just need to call them. I'm sure they just needed to get away from your little fight, and when you tell them you've made up—" He stared at them. "You did make up, right?"

They both nodded.

"Then like I said, call and tell them. They'll come home in a heartbeat. Those men adore you."

Bonnie's shoulders straightened. "I am adorable."

"As adorable as a baby pig," Henrietta said.

I stared at Dylan and held my breath.

"Always loved me a baby pig," Bonnie said.

I almost said *phew* out loud. "Dylan's right. Call them, and I'm sure they'll come home."

"We did call, they didn't answer."

"Maybe they were in a dead zone. Try again."

"What's a dead zone?" Bonnie asked.

I shook my head and then yawned. "Never mind."

"Ladies, it's late, and we're all tired. How about you two go home, and you can meet up again in the morning, say, at Millie's? Now that you're behaving, I'm sure she'll be happy to have you back."

Henrietta stretched and yawned. "I am give slap out. Carrying that suitcase wore me out. One of the men used to do that for me." She sniffled. "I miss them."

I felt like Henrietta, exhausted, but they were both more adorable than any baby pig I'd ever seen.

I hugged them each and promised to meet them at Millie's to

discuss things further in the morning. Dylan and Bo walked them to their car while I sent Old Man Goodson a text.

"Your plan worked," I wrote. "They're reunited. You can come home whenever."

I didn't expect a reply.

"Well," Dylan said as he closed the door. "At least one thing got solved today."

"What happened?"

"We arrested them all. Oh, and the outlet girl, she had a lot of nice things to say about you."

"I bet she did."

He nodded. "Told her it wasn't polite to speak of the sheriff's wife like that."

I laughed.

"Yeah, she didn't find it all that funny."

"Too bad for her. By the way, you're paying for the gloves."

"Gloves?"

"She talked me into a pair of Burberry gloves, and I'm keeping them. Consider it payment for my services."

"How much?"

I dug the receipt out of my purse and handed it to him. "That much."

"For a pair of gloves?"

"They're an expensive designer."

"I owe you that much."

"Yes, you do." I peeled off my sweatshirt. "It's so hot in here."

"Feels fine to me."

"Here." I grabbed his hand. "Feel my neck. It's wet."

He jerked his hand away. "I'll pass, thanks."

Bo followed us to the bedroom.

"So, what happens next?" I asked.

"District attorney is going for the big stuff with these guys. We checked around and found out they've got their own little ring going. Think there are at least a hundred cars in the surrounding counties."

"Wow." I spread toothpaste onto my toothbrush. "I'm glad Buddy trusted me enough to come to me." I gave him a sly smile, then started brushing my teeth.

"I already apologized, and you got a pair of gloves out of the deal."

I spit the toothpaste out. "I know. I'm just saying it's a good thing I helped, right?"

He rolled his eyes.

"What about him? What happens to him?"

"He admitted to driving his mother's car to the junk yard, Lily. He participated in the commission of a crime."

"But he also led you to the bigger criminals and a bigger bust. That's got to mean something."

"The DA is the one to decide that, but I've put in a good word."

"What about Alice Crowder?"

"No confession from any of them. We ran prints, but the gun was clean."

"That doesn't mean one of them didn't use it."

"I know. We're still working through that."

"Do you still think her husband did it?"

"Personally, I do, but the DA thinks it's tied to the car theft. We know they're working for someone, but so far, they're not saying who. I did tell Crowder not to leave town, though."

I laughed. "You've always wanted to say that, haven't you?"

"I was an Atlanta cop. I've said that hundreds of times, but it never gets old."

I walked up behind him and wrapped my arms around his waist. His strong, muscular body was tight and trim, and when I nuzzled my head into his back, it wasn't comfy. "You're a great sheriff, honey."

"I know."

"And humble."

We both laughed.

~

"That was so quick!" Belle's excitement at the success of Billy Ray and Old Man Goodson's trick showed all over her face. Flushed cheeks, wide, bright eyes, and those cute little crinkles that framed them when she smiled big. That face was the reason she rarely got in trouble as a kid. Her daddy couldn't resist it. Most men couldn't.

"And thank God," Millie said. "I was fixin' to pay for a hotel room for Henrietta myself. Don't go saying nothing, but daggum, that woman's hard to live with."

She tried to pour me a cup of coffee, but I stopped her. "My stomach's in recovery again, but thank you."

Belle eyed me, but I just said, "What," and then continued the conversation. "I checked with the contractor this morning before coming here. They should be finished with Henrietta's house by the middle of next week."

"We better pray they last that long."

"They darn well better be 'cause I ain't taking her back." Millie walked away to greet a customer at the counter.

Bonnie and Henrietta rushed in wearing matching yellow and blue striped baggy dresses.

"Oh, how cute!" Belle said. "They're matching!"

Millie didn't find it as cute as Belle. "Sweet baby Jesus, what in tarnation are you two wearing?"

Bonnie's smile was big and genuine. "I ordered some dresses from a catalog. They sent me two, so I gave one to my best friend here."

Okay, that was adorable. I got a little teary-eyed from it too. I made sure not to let Belle see. The last thing I needed was her adding that to her *Lily's pregnant and here's proof* list, because I knew she had one.

Henrietta and Bonnie stood by our table and stared at Millie at the counter.

"What?"

"Are we allowed in now?" Henrietta asked.

Millie gave them each a once-over. "You both forget to brush your hair this morning? You look like something the cat drug in."

Henrietta bent her head and narrowed her eyes at Millie. "We were up all night making a plan to get our men back."

"Did you come up with one?" I asked.

"We sure did," Bonnie said. "Now, we allowed in here or what?"

Millie took a moment before she answered. "I guess."

"Are you going to tell us the plan?" I asked.

Bonnie nodded. "We're driving down to Alabama to get our men back."

Oh dear.

CHAPTER 18

I yanked on Belle's arm. "Excuse us for a minute, please." I heaved her up and out of the chair.

She looked at me like I was crazy. "What?"

"Work stuff." I flicked my head. "*Important* work stuff."

We stepped outside the café.

"What was that all about?"

"We can't let them do that. You know that!"

She shrugged. "I don't see why not. Maybe they'll learn a lesson."

"Belle Pyott, they are not capable of driving to Alabama. They can barely drive in town, and you want to put them on Interstate Twenty?" I shook my head. "Besides, where're they going to go? They don't even know where the men are. Literally, since they're not in Alabama in the first place!"

She blew out an exasperated breath. "Yeah, you're right. Darn it. A wild goose chase would be the perfect payback for them, though."

"Remember that when we're their age."

"Honey, when we're their age, we won't be fighting over a tube of toothpaste."

"Never say never."

She crossed her arms over her chest. "So tell me this, Einstein, how're we going to stop them from going?"

I pressed my lips together. "Maybe we don't stop them after all."

"Uh, how about you try making some sense?"

A big ol' smile the size of Texas covered my face. "You could drive them."

Belle blanched, giving herself a double chin in the process. "Oh no." She waved her hands in front of her. "No. No. No. I am not going on a girls' trip with those two."

I laughed. "I was kidding. I think it's time we let the guys know what's going on. They're the only ones who can stop them from going."

"Yup. Let's just hope they survive the wrath, because when those ladies find out they've been bamboozled, it's gon' get ugly." She exaggerated her slight southern accent.

I hadn't thought of that. Poor guys.

We walked back inside, me with my head down and fingers gliding against the letters on my screen. I sent Old Man Goodson a text and let him know what was going on. He responded that they'd be at Millie's right quick. Part of me wanted to go to the sheriff's office to see where things were with Alice Crowder's case, but the other part desperately wanted to rubberneck the trains getting ready to wreck inside Millie's once again.

Millie's won. While those of us in the know waited for them to arrive, the women discussed the details of their plan.

"We got to stop at the station and ask Dylan if he can put one of those tracers on one of their cellular phones. Then all we got to do is follow it on a map. Easy peasy," Bonnie said.

Belle played along, and from the smirk on her face, she was obviously having a ball. "What're you going to do when you find them?"

"Bust a nut," Bonnie said, her shoulders up and back, her chin flicked forward.

"Bonnie!" I said, holding back a laugh.

Belle and Millie, on the other hand, busted out laughing.

"What?"

"That's not a ladylike thing to say."

"Maybe I'm not a lady after all." She winked at me. "Besides, my grandson says that all the time. He also says—"

I held up my hand. "Uh, that's okay. I know the kid. I've heard the things he's said. How 'bout we just leave it at that?"

She shrugged. "Whatever you say."

Belle opened her big, trouble-causing mouth to say something else, but I gave her a look to kill, and she shut it quickly, then mouthed, "You're no fun," at me.

The café door opened and the two most wanted men in Bramblett County walked inside. Bonnie and Henrietta jumped out of their seats. Or more like they waggled out of their seats faster than normal.

"You miss us?" Billy Ray asked.

"What're you doing here?" Bonnie asked. She immediately sat back down and motioned for Henrietta to do the same, then whispered to her, "Don't look excited. Just be chilly."

"It's chill," Belle whispered to the ladies. "Be chill."

Henrietta's eyebrows furrowed. "You're right, it is chilly. I should have brought a sweater."

"Just act like seeing them is no big deal," I whispered.

"Oh, yeah. Got it." She crossed her arms and wiggled her head like she didn't have a care in the world.

The men took their time walking the short distance to the table, probably knowing they needed to give Henrietta and Bonnie some space and protect themselves from the women's reactions.

Millie asked them if they wanted coffee, and they both said yes.

"Are you back already?" I asked.

"Just for a few days," Old Man Goodson said. "We was out looking at places to live, and I think we found us a nice doublewide just outside Montgomery. Planning on finalizing it, then packing up and heading out in a couple days."

Belle looked at Bonnie and Henrietta and coughed, but they didn't get the hint.

"Oh, wow, well, that's great," I said, playing along. "I think Henrietta and Bonnie here have something to say to you, though. Don't you, ladies?" I eyed them. "Weren't you just telling us that?"

"Oh, uh, yeah," Henrietta said. "We, uh, we made up." She hitched her thumb toward Bonnie. "The two of us are friends again."

"So you don't have to leave on our account," Bonnie added.

The entire café, which was us and four other people, got quiet, waiting for the men to say something.

They stood there, staring at the women for at least a full minute before Old Man Goodson finally spoke. "What makes you think we're moving because of you?"

"'Cause you said so yourself. On account of our fight. You said you didn't want to put up with our shenanigans."

"That's exactly what you said," Henrietta said.

"Maybe you'll consider sticking around?" I asked. "You know we'll all miss you terribly."

"Yeah, and who's going to give people sweet tea when on the ambulance, Billy Ray?"

"And the band-aids. Don't forget about those," Henrietta said.

If I had to guess, I'd say Billy Ray was Henrietta's favorite, and Bonnie and Old Man Goodson preferred each other. They liked to pretend they played alternating couples, and maybe they did to some degree, but when it came down to it, the connections were clear.

The smell of burning bacon wafted through the air, making my stomach lurch.

"Not again!" I rushed back to the kitchen yelling, "Get that bacon off that grill!"

Belle laughed. "Smells perfect to me."

Billy Ray cringed. "I like my bacon limp and greasy."

That time, I was the one doing the cringing.

Bonnie coughed.

Henrietta said, "Yeah," and coughed too. "So, you two going to stay or what?"

"Well." Old Man Goodson pulled up a chair and sat next to Bonnie. "I don't know. Lot's been happening, and the thing is, we got us some true southern belles over in Montgomery. Even wear those little hats like y'all used to when we first started spending time together."

"I liked the hats too." Billy Ray dragged a chair from the table next to us. Luckily Millie was in the back or she'd have pitched a fit about her floors. "But those ladies, they're true southern belles like the old man over here said."

Bonnie grabbed a handful of sugar packets from the cup on the table and jammed them into her large orange purse. She liked to steal them when Millie wasn't looking. "I ain't wearing no more darn hats. You got any idea how much time it takes to make my hair look this good?"

Belle shot me a look, her eyes shifting to Bonnie and then back to me.

I shrugged. Bonnie's hair was a bit of a hot mess due to their late night plotting out how they'd get their men back. Only whatever desperation they'd felt completely disappeared. They were playing hard to get, and I sure hoped it didn't work against them.

"Yeah, I'm not wearing no hat no more either. I wash my hair twice a week, and I don't want to have to do it more than that. Those curlers are starting to hurt my head."

"They have a point," I said.

Belle nodded.

The two men looked at each other. "Give us a minute," Old Man Goodson said, then leaned toward Billy Ray and whispered into his ear loud enough for us all to hear. "They look like they're gettin' along."

Billy Ray nodded. "Guess we could tell Bessie and Emma we won't be moving after all."

"Guess we could, but what if they decide to come here? That won't be good."

"No, that wouldn't be good at all."

"What'll we do then? Fussing over two women is hard enough. I don't think I can handle four."

Belle giggled.

Old Man Goodson glanced at me and winked. "Tell you what, I'll tell them you got the clap. That'll keep them from coming."

Belle kicked me under the table. I refused to look at her.

Old Man Goodson nodded at the women. "Okay, I guess we'll stay. But if you two old biddies throw any more hissy fits like the past few weeks, we're out of here."

The ladies stared at them.

"I'm not kidding around," he said. "We're too old for this stuff."

"They hear," Belle said. "Loud and clear." She stared at the women. "Don't you?"

"Aw okay. We hear," Bonnie said.

And all was well in the world of the senior coupledom once again. I said a prayer that it stayed that way.

CHAPTER 19

I tried to get a few minutes with my husband at the station, but Mary said he'd been in the interrogation room since he'd arrived.

"Oh, poor guy. I wonder if that's a good thing or a bad thing?"

"Depends on who you're asking for," she said.

I chuckled. "Good point. Will you please tell him I stopped by?"

She smiled. "I'll tell him, sweetie. How're you feeling? You're looking a little green again. You been to the doctor?"

"I'm feeling better."

"You know what it is? That flu's still going around but it only lasts a few days."

"I'm pretty sure it's just my sinuses draining into my stomach. It's happened before."

"I sure hope so."

I walked over to the office, the cool spring air feeling fresh on my skin and reminding me that I needed to spend more time outside. Bramblett was such a pretty town, and our downtown area could have been on a southern magazine cover. The women's club ran a fundraiser last fall, raising over three thousand dollars for new planters and filling them with red, white, pink, and yellow flowers. They lined the square with them, alternating the colors every few feet.

Several of the stores banded together and decided to hang white holiday lights over their entrances and windows year-round, so every night the square twinkled like an enchanted town where the weather was always perfect and nothing bad ever happened. I had a feeling someone binge-watched too many Hallmark movies and went on a mission to create their own version in Bramblett, but I was glad they did. It just made Bramblett County even prettier.

As I walked the two blocks to my office, my cell phone dinged. I dug it out of my purse and opened a message from Buddy Crowder.

I need to talk to you again.

Are you still at your aunt's? Send.

No. Home.

I told him I'd stop by in a bit. I tapped out a text to Belle and let her know where I was going, and that I'd be back at the office after lunch. She responded with a thumbs-up emoji.

I made a few client calls on my way to the Crowder house, and sent Dylan a text asking for an update. We sat on opposing sides of the *who's guilty* fence. Even though he had to pursue the possibility of Alice Crowder's murder being related to the auto theft ring, he still believed Bud Crowder killed his wife. I, on the other hand, felt her murder was connected to the car. I just wasn't exactly sure Buddy's explanation fit. Something felt off about it. Other than the fact that auto repair shops charged an arm and a leg to fix a car, I knew nothing about car parts. Were they really that valuable they'd be worth killing someone over?

Dylan once said a murder doesn't have to make sense. People kill for all kinds of reasons, and what may seem like nothing to one person could be life-changing for another. I tried to approach Alice Crowder's murder that way. Would the car's value be worth her life? Or was it something bigger, like the ring itself? Could Buddy's desire to help his family financially have led his mother to unknowingly discover a major car theft ring with ties to Atlanta? Did someone kill her to shut her up?

Or had Bud Crowder planned the entire thing? Had he heard the rumors, purposely taken his wife off the title of the home so she couldn't have it? But why, especially if they were close to foreclosure? What made me question Bud's part in his wife's murder, though, was the life insurance policy. People didn't just randomly take out large life insurance policies on their spouses, especially not ones who thought their spouse was having an affair.

Unless they'd planned to murder them.

And if that was the case, why even bother with the quitclaim deed? Just to taunt her before killing her? To let her know he was in charge and she had no power? Bud Crowder didn't strike me as that kind of man.

Things weren't adding up on either side of the guilty fence, and instead of getting closer to a solution, I was just more confused.

I arrived at Buddy's and spotted Mr. Haines outside with Hughey. He waved as I pulled to the curb. Hughey rushed over and waited for me to get out of the car. "Hey, big guy." I crouched down and gave him a big ear rub.

"You come to see the boy?" Mr. Haines asked.

"Yes, sir."

He pointed down the road. "Just missed him."

I raised an eyebrow. "That's odd. He just sent me a text and asked me to come over." I patted Hughey's head. "You don't happen to know who he left with, do you?"

"No, ma'am."

"I wonder if Bud is home?"

"You could check, but let me get inside first. I don't need that man attacking me again."

"No, you don't. It's okay. I'll just let Buddy know to get in touch later."

"If I see him, I'll tell him you're looking for him." He and Hughey headed back toward his place, but stopped before they got to his yard. "Can I give you a piece of advice?"

"Sure."

He walked back toward me. "You might want to take a step back from the Crowders. Lots of people coming and going there, and I've been hearing yelling, too. Feels like things are coming to a head, and I don't want you getting caught in the crossfire."

I nodded. "Thank you, Mr. Haines. I'll keep that in mind."

I tapped my pencil on my desk. Belle coughed. I tapped.

"Can you stop that, please? You've got me thinking to the beat of that darn thing."

My hand froze. "Oh, sorry." If it wasn't her tapping, it was me. Funny how we could do the same thing, but get annoyed when the other did it.

She wheeled her chair to my desk. "So, how're you feeling?"

"At the moment, crampy. Like I told you, I'm not pregnant. I got my period this morning."

Her pointer tooth latched onto her bottom lip as she nodded. "Oh. Well, that's a bummer."

"Sorry if I ruined your day."

"It's okay. I'll be Auntie Belle one day."

"And I promise you'll be my kids' favorite aunt."

"I've met your sisters-in-law. As if I have any competition."

I agreed and checked my iWatch. Three-thirty and my text to Buddy still said delivered. I sent Belle a text even though she was just a few feet away.

Garth Brooks's "Friends in Low Places" sang from her phone.

"Don't touch it yet, please. I'm trying something." I checked the message on my phone. It said delivered. "Okay, open it."

"Done."

I checked again, and it said read. "I don't think Buddy Crowder's read my message yet. It still says delivered."

"And?"

"When you read my message, it says read on my phone. His still says delivered."

"I think that's something you can set in your settings. He probably did it so his parents wouldn't know when he read their messages."

"What if something's wrong?"

"Like what?"

"I don't know. Just something."

She closed her laptop. "You want to go back to the Crowder house, don't you?"

"The neighbor said he's heard a lot of yelling there."

"Great. All the more reason for you to go."

"He was supposed to stay with his aunt in Alpharetta, but when he texted me he said he was home. What if someone found out where he was and…"

"Call Dylan."

"I stopped by the station and Mary said he's been in the interrogation room since he got there. And I texted him a while ago, but he hasn't responded." I checked my phone and his message still said delivered.

"I can call Matthew. I don't think you should go there again."

"I'm just going to drive by, see if I can see anything."

She rolled her eyes. "Yeah, right."

I gathered my things. "I'm not feeling great, so I'll probably just grab Bo and head home after I *drive by* the Crowder house. Unless you need me here?"

She shook her head. "I've got a showing in an hour anyway. Call me when you get home, though, okay?"

"Yes, ma'am."

I headed over to the day care. On my way, I dictated a text to Buddy asking him to check in.

The owner of the day care center greeted me at the front desk. "You're early."

"Yeah, I'm not feeling all that great and Dylan's working on a case, so I figured I'd get Bo on my way home."

"Do they have any idea what happened to Alice Crowder?"

"I think they've got some leads, but I'm not sure. He doesn't really tell me much about the cases."

"I bet he doesn't. You've solved how many now before him? His ego's probably permanently damaged."

Is that what people thought? That Dylan couldn't do his job, but some hack amateur sleuth could? Was I right in thinking I'd damaged his ego? "I wouldn't say that. Dylan works hard, and he's saved my butt a few times, that's for sure."

"You've got yourself some good timing, though, that's for sure."

A staff member walked up with Bo and released him to me. I gave him a quick ear rub and paid my monthly fee.

The owner handed me my receipt. "Here you go. All set for another month, Bo boy. See you tomorrow."

"Sure thing," I said.

Bo sat in the passenger seat watching Bramblett County roll by as I analyzed what the owner had said. "People don't really think like that, do they? I mean, sure, I've solved a thing or two, but she's right. It was just good timing, not any kind of skill on my part or anything."

Bo licked the window.

"And if Dylan hadn't been there at least a few of the times, I'd probably be dead."

Bo whipped his head my direction. A string of drool flew from his jowl and smacked onto my steering wheel.

"Ew, thanks."

He stepped onto the console and gave me a sloppy kiss.

"Thanks, Bo. Love you too."

I'd planned to drive by the Crowder house but changed my mind. I didn't want to bring Bo, and I was tired, so we headed home instead. When I pulled into the driveway, Bo whined and twisted in circles on my compact leather seat. I finally let him out, and he ran into the house like he hadn't been there in months. I walked in behind him and set my bag on the table. I was exhausted. I'd slept okay last night, but I felt lethargic, like I had no energy to do anything. I changed out of my work clothes and into black yoga pants and Dylan's oversized University of Georgia sweatshirt, planning to wait awhile and give Buddy another chance to text me. I stared at myself in my bathroom mirror. My pale complexion was even lighter, and everyone was right, I did look a little green, especially under my eyes. I dug out the bag I'd hidden in the back of my bathroom cabinet and stared at the box inside. Not possible, I thought. Not with what came to visit that morning.

My cell phone rang, so I shoved the bag back into the far corner of the cabinet and jogged to the kitchen. I hit ignore when I saw the caller ID said unknown caller. A few seconds later it happened again, so I decided to answer, thinking the tele-marketer could remove me from their list. "Hello, please remove me from your list."

"Miss Lily? It's Roger Haines."

"Oh, I'm so sorry, Mr. Haines. I thought you were a tele-marketer."

"No problem. You seemed a little worried about the Crowder boy earlier, so I thought I'd let you know I just saw him and a buddy come by the place. Don't think you have to worry. He looked okay to me."

"Thanks, Mr. Haines. I appreciate it."

My first reflex was to text Buddy again, but given what I'd heard at the day care, I didn't. Dylan asked me several times to stay out of his work, but I hadn't listened. I'd made his job worse by sticking my nose where it didn't belong, and I'd worried my husband in the process, so much that he got me a gun and taught me to use it. I'd hunted with my father and brothers before, and I knew how to shoot a hunting rifle, but the semi-automatic was an entirely different shooting style.

Being married to a law enforcement officer carried a heavy weight of worry on my shoulders. With the state of the world, especially in the United States, the risk of losing him was bigger than ever, and a day didn't go by without me praying he'd make it home safely. I hated feeling that way, hated that kind of fear. And because of my curiosity, my desire to help people who couldn't help themselves, I'd forced my husband to experience that exact pain. What did he do? He gave me an opportunity to help, something he must have thought would satisfy me. Even if those opportunities were small, even if one wasn't beneficial to the case, he'd included me. He wanted to give me what I wanted because he knew it was important to me.

And what did I do? Felt betrayed, cheated even.

I was a jerk. A big, whiny jerk who owed her amazing husband an apology and a promise to make a concentrated effort to stay the heck out of his business.

I sat on the couch, feeling awful about everything I'd done with his cases, and dozed off until Bo licked my face. I wiped the cold, wet strip of love off my cheek. "Hey, can't a girl get a few minutes of snoozing in around here?" I checked my watch. "Eight-fifteen? No way!"

Bo's lick was less about love and more about his need for food.

"I'm sorry, big guy. Momma was give out." I'd been tired, exhausted really, but didn't expect to sleep that long.

He sat behind me waiting patiently as I prepared his dinner. When I turned around to set it on the floor, there was a small puddle beneath his mouth and a long string of drool dripping toward it.

"Ew. That's just so gross."

He lapped up the dinner in seconds flat. It took me longer to clean up his puddle. I checked my phone. Four text messages from Belle, one from Dylan, and none from Buddy Crowder. That was fine. I wasn't worried. Okay, I was worried, but it wasn't my business. I told Belle I'd fallen asleep, and I texted Dylan and said the same thing, adding an *I love you and be safe* to it.

The Lily who'd just internally promised to stay out of her husband's business argued with the nosy Lily. I'd already established a relationship with Buddy Crowder. He'd confessed what he thought was the reason for his mother's death. He trusted me. I was knee-deep in the pile already, so what would it hurt to just check on the kid?

Dylan's ego. That's what it would hurt. But if Buddy was in some kind of trouble, the kid could wind up with more than a bruised ego.

CHAPTER 20

J'd done the right thing. That's what I kept telling myself as Bo and I sat on the couch. I clicked on my TV and watched a saved Hallmark mystery. I liked the Aurora Teagarden series the best, and I especially like the ones with her cutie boyfriend Martin Bartell. I'd once told Dylan if he didn't behave, I'd trade him in for Martin. He told me he'd welcome the competition. Dylan didn't get jealous, except when I gave Bo all my attention.

My cell phone rang, waking me from another sound sleep. I checked my watch. Belle calling after midnight wasn't a good sign. "Hey, you okay?" My voice sounded like I'd swallowed a sick frog.

"There's a fire at the Crowder house."

I jumped up, scaring Bo awake in the process. "What? How... how do you know?"

"Matthew was on his way home and heard the call. He called me to tell me he was heading there."

"Did he say if anyone was hurt?"

"No, but I know you're worried about Buddy."

"Yes, I am. Thanks for letting me know."

Before I could end the call, she said, "Don't do anything stupid."

"Never," I said, and hit end.

I let Bo out to potty. "Be quick," I whispered as he ambled outside. I swished some mouthwash and adjusted my ponytail, then let Bo in and kissed him goodbye. I slipped on my sneakers and headed out.

I took the shortest route I knew to the Crowder house, hearing the sirens blaring the entire way. The fire trucks, ambulance, and sheriff cruisers all had different sounds, and I'd grown to recognize them over the years. All three were headed to the home.

The closer I got, the more the air circulating through my car smelled of smoke. That wasn't a good sign. I turned onto their street only to find it blocked, so I angled to the curb and parked.

Deputy Kyle Hansen, a newer hire, stood at the yellow cone blockade. "Hey, Kyle. Is Dylan here?"

"Yes, ma'am, but the fire's bad. Sheriff doesn't want anyone past the blockade."

"Can you tell him I'm here?"

"I'll give him a call," he said, and went for the two-way radio on his shoulder.

"On second thought, don't bother." I pushed between the large yellow cones. "I'll tell him I came in from a backyard."

He hollered something as I jogged away, and I pretended not to hear. Kyle was right. The fire was bad. The entire house lit up the yard in golden-yellow, red, and amber flames. All of the front windows were broken, and flames shot out of them. Firemen stretched hoses from two trucks and sprayed at the flames. Two hoses sprayed up at the roof, though not much was left. The outside of the house, a sturdy, once-white hardiplank, remained, though the smoke and fire stained it a dark black. It was awful, unlivable, and based on what I knew about home construction, would probably need to be torn down and completely rebuilt. So much fire, so much damage. I prayed no one was inside when it happened.

A handful of neighbors gathered in the Bucklett yard and the one next to it, staring at the flames with an odd curiosity. Every tragedy was like a drive-in movie for the locals, and we'd had a run of tragedies over the past few years.

I eyed the two lawns, looking for people I recognized, and made eye contact with Stew Bucklett. "Has anyone said what happened? Is anyone inside?"

"Heard a fireman say they had one inside, and so far, no one's come out."

"Oh no."

A loud boom startled the crowd. The flames increased, and after another loud boom, the fire worsened.

I needed to find Dylan. I needed to know if Buddy was okay. Firemen crowded the area around the trucks, so I kept back, searching for a familiar body, a familiar face. I spotted Roger Haines near a sheriff's cruiser. His head shifted back and forth. The fire hadn't reached his house, and with any luck, it wouldn't. But something about the look on his face struck me. He didn't look worried. He didn't look upset. He couldn't stand still, his movements jerky and quick. He twisted around as if looking for something, for someone, and beat his fists against the sides of his hips. Haines wasn't upset. He was desperate. But why? I sped up my walk and then saw Buddy slipping past the ambulance and heading across the street. I called out to him, but there was no way he could hear me in all the noise.

Roger Haines saw him too, and he darted off, trying to catch up to Buddy. I took off in a jog after him, dodging county personnel, their vehicles, and equipment. Why was he chasing after Buddy? What was going on? From the look on Roger Haines's face, he wasn't concerned about Buddy's welfare. No. He was after Buddy for another reason.

Roger Haines killed Alice Crowder, and Buddy found out. It couldn't have been anything else.

I cut across a backyard, slowing down to climb over a chain link fence. It was dark, but the barking dogs gave me a sense of which direction to go. Roger's warning replayed in my mind. *Feels like things are coming to a head, and I don't want you getting caught in the crossfire.*

Roger Haines, I thought. Roger Haines. I squeezed my hands into tight fists as I ran. "Come on, Lily! Think!" Roger Haines knew personal information about the Crowders. The neighbors thought he was having an affair with Alice Crowder. Even her husband thought it and attacked him because of it. Was it true? Had they had another fight that led to the fire? Had Buddy been there? Did he see it?

I couldn't run and focus and call Dylan at the same time. "Siri, call 911."

"911 what is your emergency?"

I tried to catch my breath but couldn't. "This is Lily Spray—Roberts. I'm Bramblett County Sheriff Dylan Roberts's wife." I had to stop talking and slow down my run.

"Ma'am, are you okay?"

"I'm fine. Please, tell him I'm on Castleberry, heading—" I shifted my head back and forth. "Crap. Toward town, I think. I'm following Buddy Crowder and Roger Haines. They ran from the fire."

"Ma'am. What is your emergency?"

"The fire, it's the fire."

"Where is the fire, ma'am?"

"No, no. The sheriff is at the fire at the Crowder house. Just please—" I tripped and fell hands-first to the ground, my phone flying out of my hand. I rolled over on my side, pulling my left knee up to my chest. Pain burned through my leg, stabbing like knives into my knee. I rolled back over and pushed myself up as an outside house light went on to my left.

A man hollered, "Who's out there?"

I searched for my phone but didn't see it anywhere.

"What's going on?" the man yelled.

"Call 911," I screamed, and took off running, ignoring the stabbing pain in my knee.

I'd completely lost sight of Roger Haines and cursed myself for letting him get away. I stopped up the street, listened, and waited. Half the town owned dogs, so they'd have to run by another one, or I'd have to hear something, please. I had to hear something.

A dog barked, and I sprinted toward it, slowing a block up on the next street. A German Shepherd stood in the middle of the road, a street light glowing above it.

Hughey.

I spun in a circle, looking for Roger Haines, but didn't see him anywhere. "Hey, Hughey." I crouched down. "Hey, boy."

The dog ran toward me, and I dropped to my butt so he couldn't knock me over. My knee throbbed. I rubbed his ears. "Hey, Hughey. What're you doing out here? Where's your dad, big guy?"

Hughey turned in a circle and barked. "You looking for your dad too?"

He barked again.

I stood, my knee weak and hurting, and patted him on his head. Roger had said the dog was well trained and could do just about anything. I hoped that included finding his owner. "Where's your dad? Let's go find your dad."

I followed Hughey across the street and down another two, jogging through yards and between houses, my knee worse every time my foot hit the ground.

Hughey stopped in the middle of the road and stood with his head low, his back arched, and one front leg lifted just off the ground. He growled, a low, deep, scary growl. I took two steps back and ducked behind a parked minivan, peeking out around the back. Tears welled in my eyes from the pain in my leg. I breathed deeply, in and out, in and out, hoping that would help.

"You should have kept your mouth shut, boy."

Buddy Crowder walked backwards toward Hughey as Roger Haines walked toward him with a gun pointed at the boy's head.

Buddy's voice shook. "Please. I'm…I didn't know you were—"

Hughey growled.

"Hughey, stay," Haines said.

Thank God.

He stepped closer to Buddy. "I'm sorry it has to be this way, kid. Sorry about your mom too, but I did what I had to do."

I stayed as still as possible behind that car. Hughey sat a few feet between me and Buddy Crowder. I prayed the dog wouldn't turn around and acknowledge me.

Buddy pleaded with Haines. "Please, I won't tell anyone. I promise."

Haines wiggled the gun. "Afraid it's too late for that now. What's done is done."

Hughey barked.

"Quiet, dog."

He barked again and then flipped around and stood in front of me.

I kept completely still.

"I said quiet."

I didn't dare move.

Hughey stood next to the car, his tail up and firm, his backside even with the edge of the bumper.

I knew that stance.

We were on a residential street with street lamps and houses all around. Roger wouldn't just shoot the kid in the middle of the street, would he? He was out of breath, I heard it when he spoke. The chase hit him hard, and he was tired. Could he shoot Buddy and then run again? I couldn't let that happen.

I wasn't sure, but I didn't think either of them could see my shadow behind the large van. I carefully got on all fours, desperately wanting to scream from the pain of my knee making contact with the hard road, but bit my bottom lip hard instead. Buddy was only inches away from Hughey, and Haines was not even two feet in front of him. If I was careful, I could sneak around the other side of the van and maybe, just maybe, somehow get the gun out of Haines's hand. I risked Buddy seeing me and Haines turning around and shooting me, but I had to do something.

I kept low to the ground, stepping slowly so my shoes wouldn't make any noise. I checked under the van, but neither of them had moved. Buddy was still pleading for his life while Roger Haines taunted him.

"Your mother did that too. Begged me not to kill her. But just like you, it was too late. She needed to go, and you do too."

I peeked over the front of the van but could no longer see Haines. He was standing more toward the middle, giving me some leeway. I could move to their side, and they still wouldn't see my shadow.

Hughey barked.

"Come," Haines said, tapping his leg with his free hand.

The pitter of dog feet hitting the ground stopped at the front of the van. Hughey's tail wagged to a point as he assumed the same stance as before. Protective mode, ready to attack. He wasn't facing me, though, and he had to smell me. Sweat soaked through Dylan's sweatshirt. He definitely had to smell me.

Hughey wasn't poised to attack me. He was poised to attack Buddy.

I scooted closer to the side of the van, slowly lifting my body so that my back was straight. I had to do something. Buddy couldn't save himself.

My voice came out shaking and weak. "Roger, you can't do this."

Hughey backed up, wagging his tail when he saw me.

I stood with my hands out, hoping Haines would see I didn't have a weapon. I saw him through the van windows as he rotated to face the van, keeping the gun pointed at Buddy. "I tried to warn you, but you had to keep sticking your nose into my business, now didn't you?" He glanced at Buddy, flicking the gun at him. "Over here."

I charged him, pushing past Hughey and using all of my strength to hit his side hard enough to knock him down, to knock the gun out of his hand. He fell to the ground with a loud thump. My knee hit the hard road, and that was it. I was down. I rolled up on my side and saw the gun still in Haines's hand. I crawled toward it as he struggled to move. "Buddy, the gun! Get the gun!"

Buddy's body shook, and he flung to the ground, but not in time. Haines gripped the gun and dragged it toward him. He pushed at me with his shoulder, and I fell back. Hughey hadn't moved. I screamed, "Hughey, attack," and the dog hurled himself into the mix. I curled into the fetal position and whipped my body into a sideways somersault, away from the German Shepherd's teeth. The dog growled and someone screamed. The gun went flying. I crawled to it, held it up in the air, and pulled the trigger.

Hughey had Roger Haines's arm in his mouth, and Haines screamed again. "Hughey, no. No!"

The dog released his grip and stood close to Haines. He wasn't facing me. He kept his snout aimed right at his owner. I heaved myself up, keeping my weight on my good leg, and pointed the gun at Haines. I remembered everything Dylan taught me. Where to aim, how to hold the gun, where to look. I steadied my shaking hands and kept my eyes and the gun aimed at Roger Haines's chest.

The soft hum of police sirens grew louder as they approached.

CHAPTER 21

*B*elle glanced out my emergency room door. "She's coming." She hiked it back to her chair as the doctor returned to the room with my X-rays. "The good news is nothing's broken. The bad news is you're going to be off that leg for a few weeks."

"What's wrong with it?"

"You've dislocated your patella, but it doesn't require surgery, so you saved yourself a few thousand bucks." She smiled. "Orthopedic surgeries aren't cheap."

At least there was that. "So, how do we fix it?"

"We don't. It has to fix itself. We'll keep you overnight so it stays elevated, keep it iced, and we'll get you some pain meds. I'll write a prescription for you, and you'll have to do the same at home."

"I'd rather not have the pain meds."

She lifted her eyes from the clipboard in her hand. "Are you in recovery?"

"No, ma'am. I just prefer not to take them."

"Okay. How about some ibuprofen then?"

"If it's okay, I'd rather just let the pain work its way out."

"All righty then. Suffering it is." She cupped the side of the clipboard and held it against her hip. "They're getting a room ready for you now."

"Doctor, I don't mean to be a—"

"You want to go home."

I nodded.

She looked at Belle. "Can you help get her settled?"

"Yes, ma'am. And her husband should be home in a few hours."

The doctor glanced at her watch. "Works the night shift, huh?"

"Something like that."

~

Belle set me up on my couch, putting three pillows on one end for leg propping and two on the other for comfort. She let Bo out, fed him, filled my water jug, and made a snack plate. She set it all on my coffee table and scooted it near me so I didn't have to move my leg to reach. "I know you didn't want to take anything, but just in case." She wiggled a bottle of ibuprofen and set it on the table.

"Thank you."

She sat in the chair, and Bo snuggled up below her.

"You don't have to stay."

She hit the power button on the remote. "It's okay."

"No, really. I'm fine."

"Your knee is dislocated. You can't even walk to the bathroom."

"I can so. I have crutches, and besides, Dylan should be home soon."

"I'd like to stay."

"I know, and I appreciate you wanting to help, but I'm really tired, and I'm probably just going to sleep anyway. Really, go home. Get some rest, then come by later today." It was already close to seven a.m., and we both needed to sleep.

She sighed. "Fine, but if your husband isn't home when you wake up, call me, okay?"

"I promise."

After she left, I scrolled through Netflix, but nothing interested me. I couldn't sleep. My leg hurt like the dickens, and I couldn't stop thinking about what happened. Mostly because it didn't make any sense.

Why did Roger Haines kill Alice Crowder? How did the fire start? Where was Bud Crowder? Until Dylan came home with answers, I knew I'd never get any rest. Not that I could have with my knee throbbing like it was anyway.

Two hours later my doorbell rang. Bo jumped up from a sound sleep and barked.

I sat up and pushed the table away from the couch. "Just a sec." I carefully moved my leg, wincing as I set my heel gently on the floor, and grabbed my crutches from the side of the couch. "This better be important," I grumbled as I hopped to the door.

Millie smiled and handed me a paper bag. "How many times you going to get your butt in a hitch." She walked inside with a caboose of five behind her.

"Great. All y'all are here." I closed the door behind them. "If you want coffee, you're on your own." I hopped back to the couch, set the bag on the coffee table, and groaned as I put my leg up on the pillows again. Maybe I shouldn't have let Belle leave after all.

"It's okay," Bonnie said. "We brought our own." She held up her cup.

"And there's biscuits in the bag there," Millie said.

I wasn't in the mood for food. "Thanks, but I'm not all that hungry at the moment."

Henrietta grabbed the bag and opened it. "We are." She handed everyone but me a biscuit.

Bonnie proceeded to bite into hers and drop crumbs all over my floor, and Bo promptly vacuumed them up.

"We just wanted to check on you," Old Man Goodson said. The concern in his eyes warmed my heart. "You doin' okay?"

"In a little pain, and tired, but otherwise good as new."

"If new looks like death warmed over maybe," Bonnie said.

Henrietta smacked her on the arm. "I done told you not to be fresh like that."

"Telling the truth isn't being fresh."

I laughed. "I love you guys, but I'm really tired. Could we maybe catch up later?"

Millie coughed. "I think she wants us to leave."

I smiled. "Don't you have a café to run anyway?"

"The new kid can handle it for a bit."

Given the burned bacon fiasco, I wasn't quite sure.

Billy Ray bent over the side of the couch and gave me a hug. "Wish I could have been there for ya last night, kiddo."

I stretched my arms above me and hugged him back. "Me too. Your sweet tea and band-aid really make a difference. Don't ever let anybody tell you otherwise."

He nodded.

"Okay, we're outta here," Millie said. "Just come by to check on you. Now that we've all seen you for ourselves, we'll get out of your hair."

Each of them hugged me over the side of the couch, the last being Old Man Goodson.

Bonnie held the door for him. "You coming or what?"

He waved her off. "I'll be out in a minute, woman. Just wait on outside." He pressed his unshaven cheek against mine. "Time you stop putting yourself in those situations. Too many people care about you, and we don't want to see you get hurt like this again, or worse even."

"I'll do my best."

～

Dylan kissed my cheek and woke me.

It took my eyes a few seconds to focus. "Where's Bo?"

"I let him out when I got home. He's probably digging a hole in the backyard."

"He's determined to catch the moles."

"And I'm sure he will." He pushed the table aside and sat on its edge. "How're you feeling?"

I pushed myself up. "Okay, I guess." I pointed to the ice bucket on the table. "Can you get the bag out of there and set it gently on my knee, please? Gently."

He carefully placed the bag on my knee.

I hissed.

"Does that hurt?"

"It's cold."

"Ice usually is."

"Are you home for the day?" I'd taken off my watch and set it on the table, but I couldn't reach it. "What time is it?"

"It's noon. I wanted to come and check on you, but I've got to go back."

"Wait, what's going on?" My water jug was tucked between my side and the couch back. I opened it and chugged a big gulp. "Is Bud Crowder okay?"

"He's fine. Firemen got him out before the fire got bad."

"That's good." I closed the water jug and set it beside me. "Do you have some time to tell me what happened?"

"I've got a few minutes. Haines isn't going anywhere."

"He killed Alice Crowder."

"He did."

I rubbed my forehead. "I don't remember what he said. It's all kind of jumbled."

"You were right."

"I was? About what?"

"Bud Crowder didn't kill his wife."

"Haines did. He said that."

He nodded. "But the reason is the interesting part."

"He was having an affair with her."

"He was. He knew about their financial problems. Knew Alice wanted to leave her husband."

"And what? She decided not to, so he killed her?"

He smiled. "Will you let me finish?" The side of his mouth twitched.

"Sorry."

"When we questioned Dean and the tow guy, both of them said the guy who paid them was local, but they wouldn't give him up. But you know your best friend at the outlet mall?"

"It was her?"

"No, but guess who her uncle is?"

"Roger Haines."

He nodded. "Haines had himself a little car theft ring of his own. It's not tied to the one in Atlanta, like we'd hoped, but it's pretty smart for a country boy. He told Dean about the Crowders' financial problems, and Dean convinced Buddy to get the car. Promised him all kinds of cash the kid would never have seen."

"But someone slipped up, and Alice saw the car so she called the repair shop about it."

"And they called Haines."

"And he killed her to stop her from reporting it?"

"I'll give him credit. He thinks fast for a killer."

"What do you mean?"

"He told them to bring the car back, and by the time they did, he'd killed her. When they got there, he told them to leave."

"I don't understand."

"He wanted the car there in case the neighbor saw, which she did. It helped him look like a credible witness and stopped him from being on the suspect list. What he didn't bank on was you."

"Mayme Bucklett told me he was sleeping with Alice Crowder."

"Right. Put a hitch in his plan, and he got desperate."

"The fire?"

He nodded. "He needed to kill Buddy to shut him up, and wanted his dad dead to stop the rumors, so a fire was his best bet. Only Buddy wasn't home. He didn't know it."

"Buddy came home and saw him starting the fire, didn't he? That's why he was trying to get out of there."

"They had a confrontation. Buddy got away, and hid. He didn't know what to do, and when everyone showed up, he tried to talk to someone, but kept getting pushed away. Haines saw him, and that's when the chase started."

It was all so surreal. "The dog!" I started to cry. "Where's Hughey? He defended me, Dylan. He did. He knew Haines was doing something wrong, and he chose to protect me and Buddy. They're not putting him down, are they?"

"About the dog." His mouth twitched again.

"He's okay?"

"He's at the county shelter at the moment, but he's got a foster who wants him, and I'm pretty sure he'll end up a part of the family."

I relaxed. "That's good."

"The Bramblett County Sheriff family."

My eyes widened. "What? Seriously?"

"Hughey's got some serious skills. I'm not sure we'll be able to get him on board as a K9, but his foster is willing to keep him either way."

"So it's Franklin, the K9 deputy?"

"It's Matt."

If I could have, I would have jumped for joy. Bo would have that best friend after all.

Dylan helped me get into the shower, bringing me a plastic chair from the back porch to sit in. It wasn't an ideal situation, but the shower was the best one I'd had in years. He made sure I got out and dressed, and wanted to get me tucked in on the couch again, but I made him leave. I had something to do, and I wanted to do it alone. Getting the drugstore bag out of the back of the bathroom cabinet wasn't easy, but with some effort, I did.

And those three minutes were the longest three minutes of my life.

GET UP AND GHOST:
Chantilly Adair Paranormal Cozy Mystery #1

The dead in Castleberry, Georgia have a lot to say.
And Chantilly Adair can hear them.

Divorced mom Chantilly Adair hightailed it out of Birmingham, Alabama, leaving her ex-husband and over twenty years of memories behind to start fresh in her hometown.

Chantilly kept busy taxiing her tween son around town and running the historical society, but life surprised her when she took a tumble down the stairs at work.

As a result, Chantilly doesn't just work at the historical society, she now sees the history of Castleberry play out right in front of her, dead people and all.

As the town prepares for the annual BBQ competition, the king of BBQ is found dead, and Chantilly doesn't know what's worse —being the prime suspect, or thinking a ghost is the murderer.

Can Chantilly find the real killer, or will she wind up a Castleberry legend like the ghosts she sees?

**Get your copy today at
CarolynRidderAspenson.com**

KEEP IN TOUCH WITH CAROLYN

Never miss a new release! Sign up to receive exclusive updates from Carolyn.

Join today at CarolynRidderAspenson.com

As a thank you for signing up, you'll receive a free novella!

YOU MIGHT ALSO ENJOY...

The Rachel Ryder Thriller Series

Damaging Secrets

Hunted Girl

The Lily Sprayberry Realtor Cozy Mystery Series

Deal Gone Dead

Decluttered and Dead

Signed, Sealed and Dead

Bidding War Break-In

Open House Heist

Realtor Rub Out

Foreclosure Fatality

Lily Sprayberry Novellas

The Scarecrow Snuff Out

The Claus Killing

Santa's Little Thief

The Chantilly Adair Paranormal Cozy Mystery Series

Get Up and Ghost

Ghosts Are People Too

Praying For Peace

Ghost From the Grave

Deceased and Desist

Haunting Hooligans: A Chantilly Adair Novella

The Pooch Party Cozy Mystery Series

Pooches, Pumpkins, and Poison

Hounds, Harvest, and Homicide

Dogs, Dinners, and Death

The Holiday Hills Witch Cozy Mystery Series

There's a New Witch in Town

Witch This Way

Who's That Witch?

The Angela Panther Mystery Series

Unfinished Business

Unbreakable Bonds

Uncharted Territory

Unexpected Outcomes

Unbinding Love

The Christmas Elf

The Ghosts

Undetermined Events

The Event

The Favor

The Magical Real Estate Mystery Series

Spooks for Sale

Selling Spells Trouble

Cloaked Commission

Other Books

Mourning Crisis (The Funeral Fakers Series)

Join Carolyn's Newsletter List at

CarolynRidderAspenson.com

You'll receive a free novella as a thank you!

ACKNOWLEDGMENTS

This is my first book published through Severn River Publishing, and I've had such a wonderful experience with them! This book wouldn't be what it is without their help and expertise. Special thanks to Amber, the glue of SRP, and Cara my editor, who made my story read so much better than I ever could.

A big shout out to Lynn Shaw my PA, who's been with me from the start. You're a fantastic cheerleader and a good friend. And most of all, thanks to my readers. To say I'm appreciative of your support is an understatement.

ABOUT CAROLYN

Carolyn Ridder Aspenson writes sassy, southern cozy mysteries featuring imperfect women with a flair for telling it like it is. Her stories focus on relationships, whether they're between friends, family members, couples, townspeople, or strangers, because ultimately, it's relationships that make a story.

Now an empty-nester, Carolyn lives in the Atlanta suburbs with her husband, two Pit Bull-Boxer mix dogs and two cantankerous cats, but you'll often find her at a local coffee shop people-watching (and listening.) Or as she likes to call it: plotting her next novel.

Join Carolyn's mailing list at
CarolynRidderAspenson.com

65842551R00121